WE'D HAVE TOLD
EACH OTHER EVERYTHING

We'd Have Told Each Other Everything

JUDITH HERMANN

*Translated from the German by
Katy Derbyshire*

MERCIER PRESS

Mercier Press, 82c Ballyhooly Road, St. Luke's, Cork, Ireland

First published in the island of Ireland by Mercier Press, 2025

Original title: *Wir hätten uns alles gesagt* by Judith Hermann

Copyright © 2023, S. Fischer Verlag, Frankfurt am Main, Germany
English translation copyright © Katy Derbyshire, 2025

The moral rights of Judith Hermann and Katy Derbyshire
to be identified as the author and translator respectively
of this work have been asserted in accordance with
the Copyright and Related Rights Act, 2000.

The translation of this book was supported
by a grant from the Goethe-Institut.

The translator's work on this book was supported
by the Deutscher Übersetzerfonds.

All rights reserved. This book is copyright material and must not
be copied, reproduced, transferred, distributed, leased, licensed
or publicly performed or used in any way except as specifically
permitted in writing by the publisher, as allowed under the terms
and conditions under which it was purchased or as strictly permitted
by applicable copyright law. Any unauthorised distribution or use of
this text may be a direct infringement of the author's and publisher's
rights, and those responsible may be liable in law accordingly.

ISBN: **9781781178119**
e-ISBN - 9781781178829

www.mercierpress.ie

For my family

We would have told each other everything
On silences and omissions in writing
Frankfurt Poetics Lectures

WORKING ON THESE LECTURES WAS NOT EASY. On the way from their beginning to an end, private subject matter surfaced unexpectedly in my writing; we shall see whether I'll come to regret it. As will become evident, and as I expected, I have avoided writing about writing, and instead people and situations influential for my writing have revealed themselves. The first part is about the psychoanalyst Dr Dreehüs, about Ada and Marco, and also touches on families. The second part is more about families. And the third is an attempt, in the end, to bring together influence and writing.

I

SOME TIME AGO, IN A LATE-NIGHT SHOP ON Berlin's Kastanienallee, I happened to run into my psychoanalyst in the middle of the night – two years after the end of my analysis and for the very first time outside the room where I'd lain on his couch for years.

I was out that evening with G., my only writer friend. We'd eaten at an Italian place on Eberswalder Strasse, drunk a few glasses of wine together outside a bar, then G. had walked me to my tram and on the way to the tram we'd started talking about our mothers. It was that mother conversation, our slight drunkenness and the fact that we were retracing old paths – Arkona, Rheinsberger, Wolliner, streets where we'd spent our youth an actual quarter-century ago; that is, in the days when snow still fell and the world around us was black and white and pure poetry – that led me to skip one tram after another and to sit down with G. on the steps in a doorway on Kastanienallee, both of us immediately craving a cigarette even though we'd given up smoking ages ago.

A girl walked past us, smoking. I asked her for a cigarette and she apologized for not having any left, but over there – she pointed at the late-night shop across the road – you could buy single cigarettes, just like in the old days. We crossed the street, went into the shop; the Arab shopkeeper was behind the counter and in front of the counter was my psychoanalyst Dr Dreehüs, paying for a nice yellow soft-pack of American Spirit Lights.

Many times in my life, I have not recognized people when I've met them outside their usual settings. I had never faced Dr Dreehüs outside his office; nor strictly speaking inside his office. He would open the door to me three times a week; I would walk past him down the hall, enter the room, take off my jacket and hang it over the chair provided for that purpose; then I would lie down on the couch and he would take a seat behind me. At the session's end, we followed the same procedure backwards – I would get up, put my jacket back on while gazing out of the window, embarrassed, and he would walk down the hall in front of me, open the door, we'd shake hands, and then he'd close the door behind me; it was a miracle that his face, his figure and appearance had made any mark on my memory at all. In the late-night shop, I was faster than him – I recognized him first, or I realized first, and I was alert enough to find the situation remarkable and yet not give any sign that I found it remarkable. I said a polite and surprised hello to Dr Dreehüs and introduced him to G., which was amusing because they both knew about each other; G. had come up in stories during analysis sessions and had, in turn, been forced to listen to a good deal of stories about the sessions themselves.

This is G. So this is G.

G., at the end of the night and after all these years, this is in fact Dr Dreehüs, my analyst.

My former analyst. All three of us feigned bows. In my memory of the moment, I'm afraid I've lost sight of the shopkeeper, his eyes on us, on Dr Dreehüs, who seemed to be a regular customer and might not yet have revealed himself to be an analyst. Whatever the case, I embraced the curious opportunity to ask Dr Dreehüs for two cigarettes. We left the minimart, exchanged a few words, how are you, fine thanks, how are you, as he elegantly tapped the cigarettes out of the pack, offered them to us and was kind enough not to mention the fact that I'd given up smoking during my years of analysis. He seemed nonchalant, whereas I was having trouble maintaining my composure. I wanted to commit everything to memory at once: gestures and expressions, his slightly extravagant suit, the way he gave us a light, then smiled and kept a relaxed distance. I had assumed Dr Dreehüs did not exist. I had of course brooded at length about Dr Dreehüs's life outside his office and had come to the conclusion that he didn't have one, which was partly to do with him, as a professional analyst, never having betrayed the slightest detail of his existence other than his presence, his slightly dandyish shirts, ironed trousers, the interior design of his practice room and the occasional book placed as if by chance on the desk. For me, Dr Dreehüs lived in that room, with its couch by the window, its scruffy armchair at the end of the couch, its half-empty bookshelf, its empty desk. Outside that room he didn't exist. But suddenly there he was

– I lit my cigarette with the light he offered. I was aware of his hands, close to my face. I was aware that he was slightly drunk and, like me, had let loose in a sense as the night progressed. He gave G. a light too. And then he wished us goodnight, walked down the road, walked three or four metres down the road and vanished through the door to a bar – which to my mind opened solely in that instant, materializing only for him, and then closed tight behind him. Outside the minimart was a crooked bench. I had to sit down; G. had to sit down as well. We smoked our forbidden cigarettes in perplexed companionship, G.'s sympathy for my shock at the encounter consolatory. He said that he wasn't at all sure the scene had really just happened; perhaps instead it had taken place, like in a Woody Allen or Jim Jarmusch film, in a wormhole, an illusion prompted by the wine, the conversation about mothers, our wanderings into the past. The situation seemed as surreal to him as it did to me and he too had never before noticed the bar into which Dr Dreehüs had vanished like Alice into Wonderland, and when I said I absolutely had to follow Dr Dreehüs, G. said that he'd thought as much.

He said: But I'll walk you to the door, at least.

The Trommel – Dr Dreehüs's bar was called the Trommel, the drum. Front window blocked off, dim light emanating through the gap in the door, the Trommel could have been a brothel, a sex club – which I wouldn't have put past Dr Dreehüs – an Irish pub or a techno temple; we stood clueless outside. In the end, G. said: You know what, I think I'll just have a bit more of a sit-down here on the bench. Just because. I'll just hang out here for a bit longer. And if you don't come out again in fifteen minutes, I'll assume everything's fine. Then I'll go home.

He said: Is that all right with you.

I said: Yes, that's fine by me. More than fine.

G. nodded, gave me a brief but firm touch on the shoulder, returned to the crooked bench and sat down again; he straightened his back, then raised his hand like a boxing referee.

I raised my hand.

Took a deep breath, opened the door to the Trommel – and went in.

In the years after my analysis I had written my fifth book, *Letti Park*. Seventeen short stories about people between forty and fifty, perhaps at the end of their tethers and on the brink of new insights, a book that had come easily to me, written after my novel *Where Love Begins*. There had been something liberating about that return to short stories; writing it had made me happy. Looking back, I think that happiness was linked not only to the act of surviving the novel-writing process, but also to the end of my analysis, my willingness to sort things through on my own, to grow up, let go. One of the stories is entitled 'Dreams'; only a few pages long, it describes a narrator's psychoanalysis when she goes to the same analyst as a friend of hers. During the analysis the women's friendship breaks up, whereas the narrator's relationship to the psychoanalyst has a distanced constancy to it. Naturally enough, the story is closely linked to my analysis with Dr Dreehüs – that's what I write: I write about myself. I write along the lines of my own life; I don't know any other way. The character of Dr Gupta is narrated along Dr Dreehüs's lines, Dr Gupta's clothing is Dr Dreehüs's clothing, the furnishings in the office are his real-life furnishings. There is one point when Dr Gupta opens the door with a black eye, to the narrator's surprise, and that black eye too really existed. And naturally enough, that first-person narrator is me, I am her – the woman named Teresa, who dreams of slugs and elevator shafts, cries continuously, can't move for grief, can't speak in the first months of the analysis, can't possibly say what is making her sad. And naturally enough, that first-person narrator is precisely not me and nor is Dr Gupta the same as Dr Dreehüs; on the contrary, the two characters are dreams, wishes on paper, and what I imagine as I put down those words is hard to grasp. Despite the characters' fragility, what I have in mind is something unhurt, undamaged. Something I don't possess at the moment, but that I know I once possessed and may possess again, something I yearn for, an exquisite distension, a lacuna. The story is a protective space for the narrator, housing her like the shell of a nut. The narrator is the smallest doll in a Russian matryoshka, the story a cocoon round her. I don't write what she talks about, what she talks to herself about in the analysis sessions; the protective space grows out of that deliberate silence. It is up to empathetic readers to imagine it – trauma, loss, abuse, grief, absence, death and fear, life at its most normal – or to remain on the outside. It's enough for me to know what the narrator is grieving, and I'd like to keep it to myself. The story is tidy. The narrator's apartment, her everyday life, the books she reads, the paths she takes, all that has an orderly, presentable structure – in contrast to the apartment I live in, the books I read, the paths I take. I would never depict all that in a story without making alterations. The story distracts the readers from the heart of the matter; it distracts them from me. A magic trick – the readers see the magician's hocus pocus and miss the trick. I tell the story of my psychoanalysis and hand it over to a character who is the way I've always wanted to be, never was nor ever will be; never in all my life have I dreamed of slugs. And finally, the story is of course also a love story; the narrator falls in love at some point with Dr Gupta, and remains in love, and nothing changes – like I too, after perhaps five or six years of three forty-five-minute sessions a week, at some point fell in love with Dr Dreehüs and at some point fell out of love. And then it was over. And then I left him.

It came as no surprise, on Kastanienallee that night, that I walked into the Trommel with my heart throbbing.

When *Letti Park* came out, I had taken a copy to the practice. I wanted Dr Dreehüs to know he'd become part of a story in a book, that a story existed which was based on him. I knew hardly anything about him, but I did know he was a reader, he loved books. I had gathered as much from the tiny sounds of agreement or disapproval he had sometimes uttered when I'd talked about books; and I had given him the other two books I'd written during my analysis; he had read them and made restrained comments about them. I had put *Letti Park* in his letterbox on the ground floor of his practice building – addressed to him. He shared the practice with a woman with his same surname, though I could never establish whether she was his sister or his wife; I preferred the former. I had delivered *Letti Park* in person, hoping to run into him, to put the book into his hands – a brief, charged contact. Perhaps I wanted to show him I was alive. Had written a fifth book. Was doing well, was capable of going on without him; I was certain he'd be glad of it. I didn't run into him. I had put the book in an envelope with a note, three polite lines, placed the envelope into his letterbox and gone back home, and in the years leading up to our encounter in the minimart he had responded neither to the book nor to the note.

He had simply not reacted.

The story 'Dreams' has a third character: Effi, who suggests the narrator could go and see her analyst in an emergency – *if you're ever feeling bad, having a really lousy time of it* – and that character too is based on a woman I was friends with for a long time, or rather: a woman I used to know.

Ada.

These days, I wonder why I didn't give the story to Ada as well, why I didn't put a copy of *Letti Park* in Ada's letterbox in the hope of running into her. Why did I not think in the same way of Ada, without whom, in reality as in the story, I wouldn't have started my analysis. Without Ada, I wouldn't have met Dr Dreehüs, I wouldn't have written *Alice* or *Where Love Begins*; like in 'Dreams', it was Ada who'd recommended her analyst to me. Every decision in favour of a sentence is a decision against countless other sentences. Every decision in favour of a story passes up countless other stories. One word destroys another word. Writing means obliterating. I decided in favour of Dr Dreehüs and against Ada.

That's one way I could look at it.

I met Ada in the early 1990s. She was the same age as me, the uncrowned queen of a far-reaching urban tribe in which most, like Ada, came from Frankfurt an der Oder on the border with Poland. This origin, according to Ada, from a city taken by storm by the Red Army at the end of the Second World War, explained why the children of that East German Frankfurt were so incapable and full of self-hatred, so excessively unstable: Frankfurt was a traumatized city, and the people born there continued to carry the trauma inside them. Ada lived out her trauma in a large, shady apartment on Helmholtzplatz in Prenzlauer Berg, which someone had squatted on her behalf in the chaotic months after the Berlin Wall came down and which couldn't be taken away from her – for a time, at least. A huge asymmetric kitchen, wicker armchair with lambskin at the rear window, where Ada often sat and breastfed her baby. She was the first young mother I met, and she occupied her role with the air of a primordial matriarch; the wicker chair was a throne. The room full of shadows in motion, always pebbles and marbles on the long, scratched table, bouquets of branches and wild wasteland flowers in carafes, black and white photos pinned to the bare wall alongside Shiva with all his golden arms alongside newspaper clippings crackling in the draught. Candles and incense sticks, someone constantly tinkling away on the piano. The baby born in that room was delicate, rarely cried, big dark eyes fixed unwaveringly on the visitors who came and went, the front door unlocked. Inside the room there was no distinction made between day and night, the light always chalky as if underwater, no rules, barely a line to be crossed. It was evidently possible to be a reliable mother and to lose oneself at the same time, to give oneself up; I remember Ada at the counter of the bar we often went to at the time, I remember the dispassion with which she unbuttoned her shirt, took it off, sat before us with her upper body bared, upright and attentive; she wanted us to admire her breasts at two in the morning, she said they were the most beautiful breasts in all the world – and we did, and we probably assumed she was right. Where was the baby on those nights, I think these days; at the time, I never wondered about it. Ada had a husband who amazed us by managing to study law, graduate, go about a regular job, earn money and still be with us when we set out to climb down into the nights like into deep dark wells. It was Ada who pointed out to me that the family I came from, had grown up in, didn't necessarily have to stay my family, that it was possible to leave them and look for another, a better one; she had cut herself loose from her Frankfurt origins and gathered a chosen family around her, made up of her husband, her child and a close circle of other women and men. That family was good and affirming, in contrast to her biological family, whose only purpose had been to bring Ada into the world. Strangely, Ada never gave the impression while deliberating on such things that she needed any affirmation or consolation. She was invariably very composed, distanced, ironically cheerful and possessed of a defiant aloofness; she seemed always to know something I didn't. Her deliberations on the family unsettled me; as harmless as they seem to me these days, they were amazing and important to me then. My family was a cocoon in which I was pupated, bound up and safe. Ada's views tugged a thread loose from that cocoon, pulled it apart, loosened it. It was other things that then led to its dissolution, but Ada, with the baby at her beautiful breast and her husband behind her and the others behind her husband, made the first cut.

I assume she didn't know that.

When I had my baby, five years after Ada, we began to spend holidays together in my family's summer house on the North Sea. Tides and dykes, the treeless coast, the eternal triste rain were all alien to these people from Frankfurt an der Oder, Brandenburg,

East Berlin. The house, once my grandmother's home, made up for that lack of familiarity. Old, decrepit, provisionally furnished with no curtains, light perforating through the windows via a tangle of climbing plants; a fantastic uncle installed in one room who took part in our nightly parties and quoted Heine, albeit rather patchily; an overgrown garden with trees for hammocks and lanterns; and friends came and went over the weeks, extended and chosen family, taking it ever more for granted. It was that house where Ada explained her family principle to me, and she did so with a gentle gesture at everything around us. Furniture, framed certificates, turn-of-the-century photographs, stopped clocks with bent hands, chipped crockery and the name of the house, which someone had hammered beneath the gable in golden letters a hundred years ago:

Daheim: home.

All this, Ada said, is yours but it doesn't have to be. You can accept it – or let it go. You can be here but you don't have to feel responsible for anything. Anything at all. And then she stood up, walked away and left me alone with her suggestion.

I remember a dress she often wore, made of tatty indigo-blue silk and bought for ten euros at the market on Kollwitzplatz; of all the dresses I've seen, this was the most beautiful. She took it off the only time the two of us went out alone to the mudflats, as far out as possible, up to the North Sea's edge. It can't have been a coincidence that this was the one evening we spent without the others. We'd cycled to the wild beach, to the spot where the promenade ended and the dunes began. We leaned our bikes against each other, removed our shoes and walked out towards the open sea; once we reached the water, Ada took off her dress and stood naked next to me. Dusk, the sky above the land far behind us now night, the sky above the water still bright, the water mother-of-pearl, Ada's body pale and slow against the dark seam of the sea. I didn't take my dress off. She had put hers back on at some point; then we'd walked back, cycled back to the house. On another afternoon, she embraced me fiercely and unexpectedly, in the hall by the rack of rain-soaked coats, between the children's countless wellington boots, Ada's scent suddenly so perceptible, dark, sandy, almost masculine. In every one of those summers back then, Ada gave me flowers on my son's birthday, an August bouquet picked on the edges of the fields the night before; she was the only person who considered that tradition important. The summers were exhausting. Nerve-wracking, making us happy in an exorbitant way that was painful for everyone, our goals all variable and moveable, life one long lyrical transit. Once Ada's daughter was old enough to walk to school alone in Berlin, she sometimes let her husband and child return to the city without her. One summer, her husband called me after getting back home to thank me for his stay and sum up how important it had all been for him, and then he asked me to get Ada on the phone, only to tell her that the washing machine was broken and the fridge was mouldy. After that conversation, she sat down on the bench by the front door and cried. I'd never seen her cry before, and never did again. I'd like to say she left her husband shortly afterwards, met another man and had a second child; in real life, years passed between that crying on the bench and the second child, years that feel only in retrospect like a single step from one room to another. With her second child and that child's father, Ada still spent her summers at the house; we stayed close. The second child's father got the place at the head of the table; he left that spot after every meal as if he were the youngest of all the children. There was a walk on which he and Ada set out, and when they got back his glasses were broken, his shirt was ripped and his nose was bleeding. Things didn't seem to get any easier.

And yet – it's unforgettable how Ada would retire at noon with her second child, still toothless and chubby-cheeked, for a nap. How she drank a big glass of milk before the nap, the baby perched on her hip, snuggled into the curve of her arm, round cheek laid on Ada's shoulder, how she held the glass with her free right hand, downed it in one, head tipped all the way back, in deep, earnest gulps. Ritually, as if it were not milk but something far more exquisite, essential, not a drink but a colour, a material she was ingesting before she escaped with her child into the in-between world of sleep, which I knew would be deep, heavy with dreams and genuinely delicious; nothing compares to a nap shared with your own child. She put the empty glass back on the table, ran the back of her hand, her wrist, over her mouth, gave me a mysterious and tender smile, went to her room and closed the door gently behind her. In the years of her separation from her first husband, the dissolution of her chosen family, her love for the father of the second child and the birth of that child she attended analysis with Dr Dreehüs, something I didn't know at the time; she only told me about it once the analysis, the restructuring, was over. She disbanded her family. Or her family disbanded itself. The father of her first child had a baby with a woman from Tierra del Fuego, the father of the second left Berlin. The building on Helmholtzplatz was sold and its tenants were evicted. Ada moved into a small apartment a few streets away, in a building with a camera hooked up to the doorbells, which was the beginning of the end, domesticating us all.

My child got older.

The summers were limited; sometimes school resumed in early August and we had to go back to Berlin, dog days in the city, days which always made me melancholy, full of yearning for the water, the garden, the bed in the attic room with its sandy sheets, listening to my child's breathing in the night. On one of those dog days I was sitting in a cafe with Ada, and as she went to leave she said in passing that she had to go to her analysis session, one of the last. She gestured down the street towards where the practice must be. She said: A good analyst, if you ever need one.

And that was all.

That tiny scene – the cafe, the remark, the gesture in that direction – crops up in my story 'Dreams'. Two or three sentences that deliberately conceal all else – the indigo dress, the light on the mudflats and the water, the glass of milk and the nap, the chosen families, the children, mine and hers – negating it. Those two or three sentences sum up something that's impossible to grasp. They decide in favour of a single instant, a snow-globe moment. They cast all the rest overboard.

Omission.

Writing imitates life, things disappearing, images constantly left behind, falling out of focus, sputtering out. But the autonomous decision in favour of those omissions – not the glass of milk, not the dress, but yes to the cafe scene, although the milk and the dress are more sensual – makes it easier, balances out anguish and grief over loss and time elapsed. The father of Ada's second child once said that above all else he fell in love with her hands, her gestures, a remark I could instantly relate to. I always found Ada's hands even more beautiful than her breasts: their distinctive knuckles, slim fingernails, the explicitness with which she stretched out those hands, spread her fingers when she made her decisive, capricious observations, the elegant nonchalance with which she touched things, moved them, dropped them. She was a beautiful and quite cold woman with an upright, always rather defiant posture, rather defiant posture, her gait bouncy and light-hearted. I never trusted her; perhaps that's why it's hard for me to say I was friends with her. I'd rather say I used to know her. It would be easier to say I used to love Ada. After that occasion in the cafe we lost touch, I broke off contact. It may have been because I took her comment seriously, made an appointment with Dr Dreehüs, began my analysis. Too much closeness, perhaps: Ada's sessions on the couch, my own sessions on that same couch. Dr Dreehüs, I thought, knows something about me that I'd never tell him of my own accord, he knows things about me that Ada told him. I must have felt the need to regain control, to place the other at a safe distance. In the first years of my analysis I crashed, and I didn't want to expose myself to Ada in that state, have her observe me. We lost one another; I can't remember missing her. I was busy leaving my own family, and I didn't intend to start a new one.

I wanted, I think these days, to be alone.

The story 'Dreams' describes a realization – a retrospective classification of a relationship, the insight that we delude ourselves, fool ourselves, how glad we are to be fooled. Ada may have felt a vague sense of affection towards me, but she was too wary of me to let me out of her sight; I would never have become a member of her family. In the summers with the children, she always wanted us to do a group reading of Chekhov's *The Cherry Orchard*. A scene she dreamed of – the circle of friends round the long garden table by night, with white wine, cigarettes, candlelight and the classic yellow Reclam paperbacks, reading roles she'd already allotted – but it had never gone further. Those paperbacks are still on the bookshelf in the house by the sea. What would have happened if we'd agreed to Ada's suggestion? No one wanted to read *The Cherry Orchard*. Everyone wanted to drink to excess, smoke, tell stories, let themselves go, take different roles, and perhaps that was the only sign of Ada's vulnerability – that she wished we wanted to put on a play together. We didn't play together. And now our children have left home. The story focuses on the separation, a futility. Putting a copy of *Letti Park* in Ada's letterbox would have been a superfluous gesture – and beyond that, I assume Ada would prefer to leave me in the dark about her possible reading of my view of our years.

Inside the Trommel, Dr Dreehüs was sitting alone at the bar with his back to the door. The barman saw me coming and Dr Dreehüs followed his gaze, turned round to me over his shoulder and smiled – he hadn't expected me but he promptly patted the bar stool next to him, ridding me of my embarrassment. To an outsider it might have looked like we'd arranged to meet. Dr Dreehüs seemed to like being alone in the bar; we were the only customers. He smoked. The light was dim, the bar not clearly of any particular persuasion, and the slightly thuggish-looking barman seemed to sense that the encounter between Dr Dreehüs and me was – let's say, somewhat shady. A little illegitimate.

I took off my jacket, asked him for a second cigarette. Dr Dreehüs casually tapped one out of the soft-pack and held it out to me.
  He said: What are you drinking?
  He said: It's on me.

By that point in time, he and I had spent over a thousand hours of our lives together. I had talked about all sorts of things I usually kept to myself. Dr Dreehüs knew a good deal about me, I knew nothing about him, and our encounter in the Trommel was an unexpected expansion of our configuration, a small and puzzling mutation. To this day, I'm not sure whether Dr Dreehüs was a competent analyst. When other people talk about their analyses, I get an impression of lively and heart-warming communication; Dr Dreehüs, however, almost never spoke to me; I remember perhaps five utterances in ten years. The minutes passed while I spoke to myself, searchingly, pausing between my sentences, posing questions and reaching for the answers alone. These days I think that kind of analysis was exactly right for me: it was ideal.

In one of our first sessions, I had told Dr Dreehüs about my fear of no longer being able to write at the end of the analysis, having to sacrifice writing to the analysis. He had replied that that remained to be seen, and submerged after that mysterious remark into a silence from which he did not reappear for ten years. More or less. I'm exaggerating, but that is what I remember, and that is what the narrator in the story remembers: Dr Dreehüs/Gupta never said anything, and in some moments she was certain – as I was – that he'd fallen asleep. He would always sit behind me, at the top end of the couch; I would never turn round to him, having the superstitious impression that it would bring bad luck to turn round. Sometimes we'd laugh together, he had a sense of humour. Occasionally, he might express sympathy or understanding through half a sigh or a longer exhalation. But whenever I'd ask him a question he would ask me why I was asking him, and refuse to answer. There had been sessions when I'd arrived early, paced up and down the park outside the building, looked up at his windows and seen him smoking a cigarette on the balcony, and I'd felt great satisfaction that Dr Dreehüs had his own addictions, was dependent on such an unhealthy habit. He played classical guitar, the guitar leaned against his desk in an expensive bag every Monday. And that was all I knew about him. The night-time encounter in the Trommel brought with it the risk of gazing at a face that wasn't what I thought I knew. Instead, the face of a stranger to whom I had entrusted my whole life in the mistaken assumption that he understood me – and now it might prove that he'd understood nothing at all and aside from that was a know-it-all, unlikeable and cold. I was afraid Dr Dreehüs might simply not be the man I had taken him for, might, to use a preferred phrase from Ada's chosen family, be a total idiot. A *total bloody idiot*. Ten years would collapse in on themselves, crumble into nothingness:

Cinders.

Realization in time-lapse – a little more specific than the realization over years that the person you love is not the person you think they are, a gradually dawning awareness that you are alone in the world, your partner a mirror-image of your needs, a reflection which will fall away the moment you let go. Held by nothing, responsible for no one, least of all for you.

You are, in Turgenev's words, alone like a finger.

I didn't know what to drink, but Dr Dreehüs ordered for me in a manner that had a clear and absurd touch of the paternal: a gin and tonic. The barman mixed the drink placidly as I watched. And then I took the first sip, lit my second cigarette myself, turned to the side, gathered my courage and looked at Dr Dreehüs. His expression was friendly, rather arrogant in a way that was familiar for no good reason, a little weary, beneath the weariness essentially: earnest.

He was perfectly all right.

His gaze was perfectly all right, as was his gentle and mockingly interested amusement; he was nothing but a man in the late years of his life sitting at a disconsolate bar at two in the morning – on a weekday; he'd get up early the next day and go about his specific work – and that fact alone had something deficient about it, and the deficiency had something calming about it, and I had evidently not, at least not at this first glance, been wrong about him.

He said: You were brave to come into the Trommel. You were brave to come in, I'm glad, and it was clear he meant what he said.

I said: Does this barman here know what your job is?

He said: This barman here thinks I'm an electrician.

I said: I can imagine you doing almost any job but that.

As far as I remember, those were the first words we exchanged – outside, in the outside world, on an equal footing. Equals side by side at the bar, drinking, smoking. A simple routine on thin ice, reaching out our hands to each other, figuratively. It was easier than I'd expected. I asked him whether encounters like this, between analyst and client, happened often and he didn't say, Why are you asking me that; he answered straight out. He said most clients ran a mile when they encountered him in the street. These encounters were frequent. He lived next door – he gestured out of the boarded-up window behind him onto the street – his office and flat were close together, paths often crossed. His and my paths had never crossed; I would never have guessed he lived five minutes away from his office.

He said he assumed his clients' shyness was to do with shame; he was pleased to see it hadn't occurred to me to feel ashamed.

I said: It didn't occur to me, no. Actually, I just wanted to know how you read the story 'Dreams' in *Letti Park*, whether you were OK with the story.

He said: What story. And what Letti Park.

Only once have I ever encountered the woman with whom Dr Dreehüs shared his office outside in the real world. The woman who bore his name, or he hers; I didn't know whether she was his sister or his wife. I came across her in the department store on Alexanderplatz, on the floor for bedlinen, towels and pointless decorative objects, which I was only passing through because I'd been at the customer service desk, and that was where I spotted her. She was roaming in a melancholy way between the islands of piled-up towels and fluffy shower mats, and I followed her discreetly, driven by spiteful thoughts. It consoled me that this analyst had nothing better to do than waste her afternoon in a department store and spend her money on overpriced bathroom accessories, money earned by listening all day long. She was tall and heavy-set – like Dr Dreehüs – she walked with slightly bowed legs – like Dr Dreehüs

– she was his age; she could have been his twin sister. She was wearing pale-pink tights, expensive-looking, and I left her behind among the bathmats with the certainty that there was no helping her, just as there was no helping me. When Dr Dreehüs said in the Trommel that he didn't know what story I was talking about and claimed he had never found a signed book with a letter in his letterbox, there were two possible explanations for such a remarkable circumstance. Either Dr Dreehüs was lying – or his twin sister/wife had taken the package out of the letterbox, opened it, looked inside, read the letter, the dedication at the front of the book and the story and decided, for whatever reason, to make it all disappear. Even in the Trommel, I could still feel how irrevocably the book had fallen into the letterbox, impossible to take back, and now it was a question of his word against mine; in a matter of minutes we had ended up in a minor showdown.

Dr Dreehüs broke it off. He extricated his twin sister/wife from the firing line by raising his empty hands, tracing a circle with those empty hands and saying: Well, there was no way to find out now. The fact was that the book hadn't reached him, he hadn't read it but he would read it now. I was drunk enough to ask why he hadn't already read it of his own accord; it had been my first after I finished my analysis, he must have heard it had come out. He responded with a thought that I still don't quite understand to this day. He said he thought the book was not meant for him.

Every story has its first line. Not the line with which the story begins in the book; the line with which it begins in my mind. Sometimes an image or an instant, a view of something or away from something. But it's usually a line someone says to someone. I hear that line, and the hearing is accompanied by a sensation, only seconds long but clear and directly physical – a shudder, foreboding, goosebumps. There's what is said, yes. Information, claim, opinion or question, a few joined-up words, a full stop at the end or a question mark or a dash – and there's something else entirely, beneath or outside what's said, a false bottom, a hint at something I can't see, can only sense. Someone says it and is actually saying something else, and beneath it a third thing, which they themselves are not even aware of, and that passes me by and I grab hold of it at the very last moment. I pick it up, put it in my pocket. Almost a longing: to find that one story in which a character can say this line to another character, and linked to it, a fixing of the sensation, and linked to that perhaps, a moment of understanding. Not closure but convergence. The things we did and thought years ago that suddenly, like in a long-drawn-out sound wave and utterly unexpectedly, point to an outcome; and no matter how remarkable, it is a result.

So there's this first line in my mind. And then the search for a place for that line and at some point a character who can actually say it, and another for whom it can actually be meant. And then there's the table the two of them are sitting at, the room in which the table is set up, the house in which the room is, which one of the two will leave and almost certainly not come back to. So much golden snow in the light falling through the doorframe. Every time a story is told, John Burnside writes in *What Light There Is*, it is being told for the first time; or to put it differently, as Christoph Ransmayr writes, stories do not transpire, stories are told; and differently again – as Lars Gustafsson writes – all these things that accumulate over a human life.

Load them up with meaning.

During the years I laid on Dr Dreehüs's couch,

I told him about myself or talked about myself; call it what you like: ultimately, I was telling him stories.

Don't you go telling me stories.

My family's stories – those that were told to me, and those I was not told but guessed at. My own stories, which don't belong to me at all though, which are nothing but an unclear trail from a long-past uncertainty via the here and now to a questionable later. I did my talking in analysis, it occurs to me, in the same way as writing a story. I made a start and from there I beat a path into one of yesterday's thickets, and then I turned back, without reaching a conclusion, from the thicket via the start into a present day, which is connected to everything that once was.

I can point out that first line for every story I have written. I can find it again: the core, the smallest matryoshka doll at the nub of the story, told with the intention of showing it and simultaneously concealing it. I can find the line again – that's not right: I know it, and I keep it to myself. When I talk about it at events, there are readers who say they've found the line. That makes me happy. It means the story has detached itself from me and transferred to somebody else. A dybbuk. A pale dybbuk that someone else but me wants to question, a shared riddle. Sometimes I'm brave enough to ask the reader to show me the line they've found. Sometimes I don't ask. This hesitancy is mutual; most readers say they've found the line but then keep it to themselves. They have the same intentions, following the same circuit of revealing and concealing. Only in the story 'Dreams' about my analysis years can I not find that line – I no longer know what it was. Either it never existed for the story, or it is now obsolete. Or perhaps something happened that is actually not possible: I hid it not only from the reader but also from myself, which would make a mockery of my entire analysis – a thought I am perfectly comfortable with.

During the first weeks, perhaps months, perhaps for the whole first six months, I lay on Dr Dreehüs's couch and didn't say a word. I had tried to say what I wanted during the first session. In the next, I said nothing. I had entered his room, lain down on the couch, folded my hands over my stomach and said nothing, until Dr Dreehüs said: Well. The session is over for today. He did not interrupt my silence, never told me to speak, never asked me why I was silent, he never made a suggestion. He did not come to my aid.

At the time, I thought: he's not coming to my aid. Now, I think he perceived my silence as a search for a beginning – and presumably, it was. I was sorting through the stories, my own and other people's, I was looking for the first lines and deciding: what do I want to tell, and what would I rather withhold. I was securing myself and the actual stories; only then, much later, did I start to speak. If I write the way I spoke in my analysis, or vice versa, if I spoke in analysis the way I write, then I always kept back the actual core of the matter. And if that were the case, then Dr Dreehüs stayed silent, never spoke to me, never asked a question, never gave away an answer, so as to leave me that actual core. So that I can go on writing.

In the Trommel, Dr Dreehüs said what he'd never said in our ten years together – he ordered us a second gin and tonic, offered me another cigarette, and the bored barman mixed the tonics and shifted the stool he was sitting on behind the bar a little closer to us – Dr Dreehüs said: How are you doing.

And I said, without hesitating: Fine. I'm doing fine.

And that's how it was. I was doing fine sitting at the bar of this place, which G. had said he'd never seen before and he was convinced it would no longer exist when he walked down Kastanienallee the next day. It would have disappeared back into its wormhole, it had only existed, along with its barman, cigarettes and tonics, for this one encounter, and I knew the fifteen minutes that G. had said he'd wait for me were long since over and he'd gone home; that he was thinking of me, I knew that too. I could have quizzed Dr Dreehüs a little – calibrated this or that suspicion beyond the information that he lived only five minutes away from his office and sat around in bars at night. Did he come from the West or the East. Was the other Dr Dreehüs his wife or his sister? I asked nothing of the sort. It was a little as if we were caught in that special, focused, frosty spotlight of a short story, which begins somewhere, captures something, breaks off again before it can come to its conclusion. I know something about the characters in a story when I write them, I know everything, basically: birth, origins, childhood, growing up, their age and their secret, but it's not necessary to specify that; quite the opposite. It gets in the way. It blocks the view of the essentials, the concentration on the moment. I wanted to leave my speculations about Dr Dreehüs out of focus, so as to sit at the bar with him in this wonderful, slightly seedy and also playful way, and he seemed to see it similarly. And so what we talked about over our second drinks did not go particularly far. We simply sat together and smoked, and sometimes he smiled over at me, and I smiled back.

He said: I thought so.

I said: What did you think.

He said: I thought you'd be doing fine. I didn't worry about you.

I said: You didn't think about me.

He considered that for a moment, and then he said: Yes, perhaps I didn't think about you. I was sure you'd be all right, and perhaps you really did leave at exactly the right time.

It was me who had ended the analysis, not Dr Dreehüs. I had ended it fairly abruptly. Perhaps I'd hoped he would hold me back, but he hadn't, of course.

I said: And why were you sure I'd be all right.

And he said: Because despite it all, I always found you slightly self-pitying.

During my analysis with Dr Dreehüs, I had cut my ties to Ada. The ties to the members of her family, her tribe, had remained fairly intact, at least to the more distant members, the people in her outer circle; that included my ties to Marco. Ada liked to compare us to a wolf pack, which was not much of a stretch; our pack had its alpha wolf – or alpha she-wolf – and other wolves close around her – betas – plenty of them, and then there were the gamma wolves who circled the pack, couldn't live with it and couldn't live without it.

I assume Ada saw me as a gamma wolf.
Marco was a gamma too.

He came from Frankfurt an der Oder, like Ada, and they'd known each other since they were children. They'd lived in the same neighbourhood, gone to the same kindergarten and the same school to begin with, but Ada had stayed on until she was eighteen and Marco had left at sixteen and had to go straight into the army. Then the Wall came down and both of them moved to Berlin, both more or less breaking off contact with their parents. Marco lived in a one-bedroom flat in a high-rise; it was sometimes impossible to set foot in there because he had a tendency towards squalor and would withdraw into himself, not want to see anyone, stop doing things with the rest of us. Then there were times when he was distinctly vital, sociable, communicative, would host big surprise meals; he loved cooking and did it well, he was generous and could be warm and caring; then that would break off again and he'd disappear for months at a time, only to pop up again unexpectedly, to be there. Now and then his mother turned up from Frankfurt, bringing a basket of chanterelles and home-baked bread. He'd let her into his flat, she'd clean it up and head back home. His relationship with his father was more difficult. Marco would hide from him; his father would turn up at all the flats where he suspected his son might be, leave a twenty-mark note on the kitchen table and go back to Frankfurt without finding him; we'd buy beer and dope with the money and call up Marco and say: He's gone, you can come out now. Marco had various artistic ambitions. He wanted to be a director, make movies; he applied to film schools with three short films and was roundly rejected by every one of them, then put together a portfolio of drawings in two days, applied to art school on a whim, and they took him right off the bat. His pictures were sexually charged, disturbing and violent, and then again poetic and quiet in a withdrawn way. He was a huge man with extraordinarily good teeth, dark lips, eyes that were indeed wolf-green; he rarely washed, always wore the same clothes, drank and smoked exorbitantly and wanted nothing from women except anal sex; he had a specific way of pronouncing the words *big breasts*, as if they were something edible; Ada summed him up as a maximum-security unit to which someone had long ago thrown away the key.

In the summers, he came along to the house by the sea. He was the only man who wanted to cook for everyone, wastefully sumptuous dishes with fish and meat; he was obsessed with shrimp, bought them fresh off the fishing boats and peeled them with the children on the patio outside the kitchen, leaving the ground covered in their pale-pink shells that crunched under his bare feet. He'd boil up the shrimp for days and work with the stock, that's what he'd say – 'I'm working with it.' He never wanted to sleep inside the house. He'd put up a camp bed in the shed and hang a hammock between the plum trees on hot nights; if we begged him for a really long time he'd play the guitar and sing along, preferably 'Buenas Tardes Amigo Hola My Best Friend'. At the end of his course he wrote a thesis with the title 'I Am the Bullet in Kleist's Head', which was rejected; but he didn't care, he just left art school without a degree and got his first exhibition in a gallery in Berlin Mitte. On the day after the opening he turned up at my front door and the left half of his face had somehow slipped out of place, his mouth drooping down at the corner, his eyelid drooping, the eye half-closed; he looked like he'd had a stroke. We went to the doctor, who suspected facioplegia, facial paralysis due to stress. The paralysis went away again but there were other symptoms, tingling in his legs, disturbed perception, tremors, fatigue and unfounded aggression, a strange kind of dopeyness when dealing with everyday situations. Marco consulted another doctor and then another and a fourth one, until eventually he got a diagnosis: multiple sclerosis, pretty far advanced.

He gave away his pictures, cleared out his studio in Monbijoupark and withdrew to his one-bedroom flat. He put a brazier out on the balcony and asked visitors to bring firewood. When I visited him we'd sit by the fire on his balcony and look out at the grass behind his high-rise, at communal washing lines and blackbirds; amazingly, his neighbours took no notice of the fire on the balcony, just ignored it.

The fire was Marco's tribute to the things that had been important to him, and at some point he gave that up as well, leaving a sooty stripe on the pale wall of the balcony, marking the spot where he'd leaned when he'd put out the embers at dawn and gone to sleep. He stayed in his pyjamas, got meals on wheels, drew the curtains and switched the TV to the cartoon channel. He walked towards his illness, went right inside it, like into a forest or deep water or a vacant, abandoned house. There were a few attempts to persuade him to try medication, speech therapy, occupational therapy; in vain. He quickly weakened, was soon unable to walk and had trouble speaking, holding on to things, eating without help, and in the end his parents came, took him back to Frankfurt and didn't think twice about putting him in an old people's home.

I visited him a couple of times in that home. It was a sixty-minute train ride from Berlin; the home was right by the station. They separated men and women, the men sat in one day room, the women in another, and there were no shared mealtimes either, so Marco had decided not to leave his room any more – he wasn't interested in eating with old men – and the management had accepted it. Marco stayed in his room, and in his room he stayed in bed. I visited him for one or two hours and we stared together in silence at the TV, where the cartoon character Yakari rode a wapiti deer across a grass-green plain; then I set off again and took the train back to Berlin. Perhaps a year after he was admitted, he came down with a bad case of pneumonia and had to be intubated. He was awake and conscious, and the doctor treating him apparently asked him whether he wanted them to continue the artificial respiration, meaning Marco might have survived his pneumonia and been taken back to that room, and Marco apparently asked them to stop the artificial respiration, which the doctor did. Marco died in the early-morning hours of one of the first, often so fragile days of January. It was his mother who called to tell me and at the same time to say that they didn't want anyone from Berlin at the funeral. None of his friends were to come, the family wanted to bury their son with immediate family only. Marco belonged to the family, they said – and not to his so-called friends. It had been his so-called friends, ultimately, who had let him get sick.

There must have been people who talked to Marco's parents about it. He had a lot of friends, and although most of them had withdrawn during the years of his illness, they had loved and admired him and many of them felt the need to have what we call under these circumstances a final farewell. The family eventually agreed to have Marco laid out and to let us view him in his casket; in return, we had to promise to stay away from the funeral itself later on. We headed for Frankfurt an der Oder on a grey winter morning – sharing several cars, a sad procession – and stood outside the funeral parlour on the edge of the city, in a long queue outside the room where Marco was laid out. Without having discussed it, we went into that room in twos and threes, depending on our states of mind, fear and sadness, and I think I went in with someone who left before me, left me alone with Marco for a few minutes. The illness had taken away his weight, his hair had grown sparse, his large hands now thin. Having visited him in the home, I was not much shocked by his fragility; perhaps that fragility had been visible in his healthy years as well. His parents had dressed him for the casket. He was wearing clothes he would never have worn when he was alive, a neatly ironed checked shirt with a stiff collar, over it a cardigan with a zip and a maritime crest, his thin hair wet-combed into a parting.

He looked like the man he might have become if he'd stayed with his family – if he hadn't met Ada, hadn't followed her to Berlin, hadn't come across the others in Berlin, if he hadn't heard Ada preaching that you can leave your family – and in the end, his family had taken him back and showed us who he belonged to.

Who he belonged to at the end, at least.

I don't remember touching him again in that room.

I remember the expression on his face, a face still familiar to me now: closed, controlled. Absent.

From the undertakers, we drove to a factory on the River Oder where someone had hung Marco's pictures; the footage from his film school applications was projected onto the rough walls in infinite loops, in which he practised major self-harm and had persuaded various people to let make-up artists glue their eyelids shut in long strenuous sessions and to reveal their genitalia to the camera. We stayed a long time in the factory even though the heating was broken and it was freezing cold, not driving back to Berlin until the shelter of darkness descended. A few days later, I walked into Dr Dreehüs's office at the usual time, didn't take off my coat, didn't lie down on the couch, but sat down on the chair beside the couch and said I wanted to end my analysis. It was over.

Marco's laying out had balanced things. It had been so terrible that my own horror, my pretentious and, as Dr Dreehüs called it in the Trommel, my self-pitying sorting and questioning of the events that had been difficult in my life withdrew: my horror gave up. I gave up wanting to put names to these things, to control them; there was simply no point any more. I had the impression it was all about anticipating, accepting – sadness, memory, the unreliable and mutable aspects, and the first step after this unexpected insight seemed to be to stop all my talking and wrangling.

To break off, to walk out.

Dr Dreehüs had already sat down in his armchair at the head end of the sofa and put on his analyst face, the face I had perceived out of the corner of my eye in the countless hours that lay behind me, while I'd taken off my coat, put down my bag. Too briefly to grasp it, long enough to understand that it was a mask, not in a negative sense, but directly: the expression he assumed when engaging with his client, eyes downcast, mouth frowning, concentrated, and underneath it, or so it seems to me now, definitely on the alert. Now he looked up at me and the mask slipped. I could see how surprised he was, and I could also see that my announcement hurt him. I raised my hands and tried to say something; he knew about Marco's death, the laying out, us being banned from the funeral. I tried to say that I'd reached the end of a conjecture, didn't yet know which way next; but I couldn't get to the point, and ultimately I didn't care by then whether he understood me or not, whether I could express what I wanted to express or whether I and my words failed. It didn't matter. We sat together for those forty-five minutes, opposite each other like the very first time. Dr Dreehüs, as always, said nothing. And I said nothing more either, and after the forty-five minutes passed we stood up simultaneously, shook hands, and I left his office.

I remember the moment I crossed the threshold. It was like in the recurring dreams of my childhood; the floor might have given way under my feet, the walls of the corridor might have dissolved and transfigured into something rubbery, fluorescent, the stairs might have started swaying, moving apart. Nothing like that happened. I simply crossed the threshold and went down the stairs, out onto the wintery midday street. And never went back.

In the Trommel, Dr Dreehüs said that word – self-pitying. And although it took me by surprise, I agreed with him and I still do. It's a good word, and it sometimes helps me to get over myself. I'm not sure whether Dr Dreehüs knew that, whether he might have given it to me to take home: a word like a talisman, a protective word.

Self and pity.

I didn't have a third gin and tonic. Dr Dreehüs assured me he would buy my book; he definitely didn't want a second copy in his letterbox; and he promised to get in touch once he'd read the story 'Dreams'. He said the drinks were on him and I thanked him, said goodbye to him and the barman, stepped out of the Trommel and back into the world. It was early morning but it was not yet really light, for which I was grateful. I walked all the way home, from Prenzlauer Berg to Weissensee, and I was extremely happy. It's hard to say why I would have been unhappy if it had turned out that Dr Dreehüs was a total idiot; it wouldn't really have changed anything about my ten-year monologue. But it seemed to have turned out, unexpectedly, that Dr Dreehüs was perfectly all right, that he had known or recognized at least some of the feelings I'd expressed, that we had communicated with each other after all. How can I tell? It's rather like deciding on a story – how can I tell that a story is a story. That a word, a line or an object might be the start of a story, a plumb line I let down into a deep well. What am I relying on there? I suspect I'm relying on a specific instinct. On the one instinct that tells you something is missing, not that something is there. That expression we sometimes use – *do you know what I mean* – we say it when we don't know how to go on, and it's always an evasion, a tacit agreement; even if I don't really know what you mean, I do get a sense of it, or rather: I'd like to know. And perhaps that's enough. I'd like to rely on there being some form of understanding, of shared knowing and perception. And even though I think I know that each of us remains alone, it still seems important to me to want to change that, in the face of all reason and until the very end.

A while after my night-time encounter with Dr Dreehüs, three or four months later, Ada turned fifty. Had I not encountered Dr Dreehüs, that fiftieth birthday would presumably have passed me by; I'd have thought of it but it wouldn't have occurred to me to congratulate Ada. The encounter with Dr Dreehüs had shifted something, brought it to an end and a new beginning, and because that had a long echo I found myself, on that evening in early December, outside the building where Ada still lived.

And as I write this, thinking back to that day, I'm not at all sure it really happened. Did I visit Ada? Or did I dream that I visited her. Or did I think about writing a story in which a woman visits another woman after encountering their analyst in the middle of the night; was I looking for the thread that could lead to one person hugging another person she hasn't seen for ten years, on the threshold of an open apartment door. In retrospect, I'm sometimes not certain which part of a story happened and which is made up, which part harbours the so-called autobiographical truth; though that makes no difference at all in the end. Had I written a story about a visit like this one, the beginning of the story would have been an object: a guitar. So if I assume I really did hug Ada on her fiftieth birthday, then I hugged her because my son had asked me to take his guitar home with me. I'd met up with my son, who was coming from a band rehearsal and wanted to go out for the night but his guitar was in the way; we had shared a hurried rice dish at an Indian restaurant, I had equipped my son with all my usual pointed and pointless warnings, then I had let him go, walked home with his guitar on my back and thought out of the blue of Ada. Of her birthday. Of the years. I had thought, now's the perfect moment, and I'd turned round and gone to her. The guitar on my back was part of it. It made me not quite myself. I was slightly someone else, a musician on the face of things; perhaps I was on my way home from a gig, the instrument's weight on my back reassuring me, the feeling I could be someone else relieving some of the pressure. And as well as that: my son was grown up, there was so little I could still do for him, so it was comforting to be able to carry his guitar home, at least, if I could no longer look after my child as he set out on his wild journey. I was open-hearted on one hand and wistful on the other, I felt protected by the guitar as if it were armour, and under that protection I pressed Ada's doorbell and waited for the buzzer to sound. I left the light in the stairwell off, a detail I would mention without explanation in a story, and ascended the three flights of stairs to Ada's flat, where I had once been so often but at this point not for years.

What had I expected.

I had tried to prepare myself for her not letting me in. I had imagined a number of guests, rather complicated combinations, people from the inner pack whom I hadn't seen for years. I had assumed I'd have to deal with the kind of looks people give each other when they're getting older and haven't met for a long time, the disdainful or approving scrutiny of the ageing process, the other person's visible relief that you too, and so forth; I had reckoned with Ada's typical cold atmosphere beneath her initial cordiality, and I was intending to drink one glass of alcohol swiftly and then another. All my assumptions were wrong. Ada was home alone. She stood in the doorway and peered into the dark stairwell, saying a cautious who is it; arrived on her landing but still in the dark, I said my name; she hesitated for a fraction of a second. And then she took a step back, repeated my name, opened the door wide, asked me in, and we embraced.

Word had got around that Ada was now living with a woman. I would have liked to see the woman, especially how they were together, but she wasn't there. They'd argued and the woman had moved out on the morning of Ada's birthday. Ada didn't seem sad about it. She'd moved out, but she had given Ada flowers: irises, thistles and lilies on the kitchen windowsill, the only sign of a possibly special day. There was no party. No guests, no food, no champagne in buckets, no private concert, no music to speak of. Ada was simply sitting in the kitchen, drinking a beer out of the bottle. In the next room her second child was playing a computer game with the door closed, audibly involving a lot of guns, and in Ada's bedroom her older daughter was lying in bed, having chosen her mother's big day to have her wisdom teeth pulled. I sat down on the edge of the bed next to Feli for a while, put my hand on her swollen cheek. Had she not had her wisdom teeth pulled, she would have been out and about on that wild journey with my son; our children had ended up friends even though we were no longer friends, or perhaps for that very reason. The children were still attached to those summers, the communal structure in the house by the sea; by all appearances they wanted to continue it, couldn't let go of each other, unlike the adults. If Feli was surprised by my appearing, she didn't show it. She held my cool hand for a while, then let go. I went back to the kitchen, where Ada had put a beer on the table for me. The kitchen was unchanged, the same exquisitely careless chaos as ever; only the photo booth strips on the fridge were new, and the door had been painted as a blackboard, on which someone had chalked the words: *It's bright enough to see that it's getting dark.* The bookcase still on the back wall – twenty-five years back, I'd been impressed that Ada kept her books in the kitchen – and round the vase on the windowsill lay the things that had fallen into her hands, things to which she had lent value and meaning, until she'd drop them from one day to the next; that evening, a stone with a hole worn in it by the Baltic Sea, a wooden fish, Jaxon-brand chalks. The walls between the bookshelf and the sink were still covered in her second child's wax crayon scribbles from the skirting board to about a metre up; of course she'd let her second child draw on the wall, she'd practically encouraged it. Over the past few weeks, Ada told me, he hadn't felt like going to school and she wouldn't force him in any way; now his father had sent the child welfare people round and the whole thing was getting stressful. Ada didn't look like the whole thing was getting too stressful, and she told me about all these disputes as if we'd last seen each other a week before.

Familiarity.

We sat at her familiar table by the window with its view of the backyard and the brightly lit windows of other people's lives, and raised our bottles in a toast – all the best for your birthday – and despite all this familiarity we were still touched, moved in a slightly embarrassed way. We told each other this and that, then we got on to the summers; she asked how the house was, and my uncle, asked a little about my writing, but we took it no further than that. I told her nothing about running into Dr Dreehüs, which Ada would certainly have found extremely interesting; I kept it to myself. Nor did I tell her anything about the story 'Dreams'. I was pretty sure Ada had read it, and if she'd read it then she knew I'd got over her.

She seemed to know I was over her.

Feli came into the kitchen, warmed up a jar of baby food and sat down with us, a graceful girl with long limbs, blank eyes; she had obviously already learned that you can fall out of touch for half a lifetime, then you see someone again and pick up where you left off, you simply continue – yeah really, you do. The years between don't matter; people update and uphold themselves in your life, whether you see them or not – it doesn't matter. The younger child interrupted his excessive computer violence – Ada emphasized that it was a game, her younger child was playing one way or another, and who would deny that to a child – came into the kitchen and helped himself to a piece of cheddar out of the fridge; unfortunately he closely resembled his father, seemed absent, indifferently proffered a weak handshake and went away again. When he was four I had given him a toy gun for Christmas, and he'd instantly shot his mother dead without a moment's hesitation, as if he'd just been waiting for this gift; we hadn't seen each other again since. Ada used to carry him up the stairs to his kindergarten; when another mother asked her why she was still carrying such a big boy, she answered: Because I love him – an answer I think of whenever I get caught in the turbulences of nearness and distance with my own child, when I have to let him go, trust him, trust fate. Ada's second child seemed safely harboured in this flat with his mother and sister; that was certainly a good thing, and yet it would presumably not make his life any easier. Who am I to judge. I looked at Ada; she looked beautiful, her hair was black and silvery, her unapproachable expression intensified, her distance as if hemmed in. I looked at Feli and watched her younger child leaving the room, and Ada let me look; a few weeks before, she had been to my son's very first gig as the front man of his band, performing completely wasted, a gig I had good reasons not to attend – Ada and I had nothing to hide from each other in that respect.

I stayed until midnight. Then I shouldered my son's guitar again and we said warm and quite intimate goodbyes. We've had no further contact since then.

The truth.

I swear to tell the truth, the whole truth, and nothing but the truth. When I was in my early thirties I once said to Ada, in a bar at half past three in the morning, that I wanted never to lie again, and she laughed for an incredibly long time. The man I was married to all the way through my analysis had his own view of my night-time encounter with Dr Dreehüs. I didn't tell him about it the next morning; not until several months later. The next morning, I answered his question about my night out with G. evasively and kept my encounter with Dr Dreehüs to myself, hoarding it jealously like a fairy-tale dwarf hoards his precious stones, his treasure. It was a treasure, I didn't want to share it, and I probably knew what my then husband would say about it. I suspected. Months later, in a moment of weakness and trust, I did tell him about it, in a *Do you know what I want to say* moment. He didn't know what I wanted to say, or he knew it better than I did. He claimed that at heart I was interested in nothing other than going to bed with Dr Dreehüs, a plan linked to the fact that I'd actually wanted to go to bed with Ada, and the encounter that night in that bar had been the ideal coincidence for my intentions. And only because I was astonishingly wiser than my desires had I stopped at two hours at the bar, gin and tonic and cigarettes. Dr Dreehüs, he said, had pointlessly prolonged my analysis for ten years to find out whether I'd go to bed with him, although he was actually more interested in men, which my husband claimed to know because, unlike me, he had once run into him outside his office, and in so-called real life Dr Dreehüs had given him a look that was absolutely unmistakeable, according to my husband.

Fine.

I'll just leave that here. It doesn't actually matter, I'm just adding it to all the rest because it casts more light on things. Ultimately, there are always several reasons for everything we do – those that we know of, and those we suspect. And those we know nothing of. And the latter may well be the strongest and the most compelling.

A few weeks after our encounter, Dr Dreehüs wrote me a short, friendly letter. He wrote that he had had the pleasure of reading 'Dreams' several times. He wrote (I quote): *What untiringly detailed work, altering and distorting everything so skilfully that in the end nothing is correct any more, yet everything is true.*

And he added: *It would be nice to hear from you, Ms Hermann.*

II

I HAVEN'T WRITTEN A STORY ABOUT MY encounter with Ada on the night of her fiftieth birthday. Perhaps I have written a draft here, discovered the start of a story I might one day write. Perhaps, though, this piece renders a potential story about a fiftieth birthday redundant; it is often the case that I perceive things, once brought into the light, as sacrificed and lost. The story about the night of Ada's birthday, were I to write it, would be less about those hours in the kitchen, and more about us not seeing each other again afterwards. The story would not tell that part, but it would have to end by establishing that fact. That is the centre of the story: what doesn't happen, what's lacking. The omission.

The omission, as always, in fact, would be the crux of the matter.

Nor have I written a story about Marco's laying out in the funeral parlour on the outskirts of Frankfurt, or about our nights on his balcony with the view of his neighbourhood, or a story about my visits to him in the home, the hours by his bed, which left a deep impression. During one of these visits, Marco had said out of the blue: I'm a king – a line typical of him, which I didn't question; he was right. In that bed in that grim room with its TV, the empty Formica table by the window, the wheelchair he never used because he never left the room and the family photos his mother had put up on the wall above the bed, nailed to the wall so he wouldn't forget where he came from, he was a king. No story about Marco, even though lines like that one have stayed in my mind, so obvious for the dark magic of a story that they're almost irresistible. But unlike the questionable encounter with Ada on her birthday, I am horribly certain that Marco's laying out took place. The year in the old people's home took place, the farewell took place, and that's why I haven't written a story about it. Marco is gone. The gap he leaves is not theoretical here, not romantic, it's not my or his decision; it is a plain fact. There are sentences that are too close to real life. They belong to real life, are impossible to separate from real life.

They don't have a secret.

They are clear, a form of truth, there is no doubt about them. Lines that lead into a story come from the in-between world; they are shifty, open to interpretation, open to change, which means the world is open to change. I can change the world, my world, with a story. Two pages. Seven pages. Melting points. What light there is. That's what I think I know. And beyond that, there is of course what the stories know and what they decide without me, over my head. I might write a story about Marco's laying out much later, write my way around that laying out, write around its margins. That story might already exist, I just can't see it yet. I could say – I'm still dreaming it.

Dr Dreehüs had given me instructions for dreaming. A suggestion. Write down the dream the morning after you dream it, set that version aside, write the dream down again the second morning, and then a third time on the third morning after the dream. Only then, look at the three versions side by side and compare – the detail that goes unmentioned in the third version is the detail for which the dream was dreamed.

Does this procedure hold water. Is it officially approved, or did Dr Dreehüs think it up for me.

Either way, it occurred to me when I read his letter. His impression of my work, the thought that at the end of the story nothing is correct any more, yet everything is true. The untiringly detailed work of cutting, as if there were parallels between working on writing and working on dreams.

I've rarely used this kind of dream interpretation; I dream too little. Dr Dreehüs will have been disappointed by my lack of dreams – a line that occurs in the story: *disappointed in her because of this lack of dream material.* I might call my tendency to encapsulate sentences, my need to weave a cocoon round a moment, an imprint from my early childhood. I don't dream because I'm already constantly occupied with hiding things, keeping them at a distance. Or the opposite – perhaps I don't dream because I write.

When I think of my childhood, Guntram Vesper writes in *Lichtversuche Dunkelkammer, I remember experiences as ciphers, which decode what occurred around me and happened to me.* In my case it is the reverse – experiences are ciphers that encode what happens around me, break down its boundaries, multiply it, float it and in the end simply dissolve it, still not understood.

During my childhood, I dreamed a dream that left such a strong impression that I recall it to this day. The dream is linked to the doll's house my father made for me, which I played with a lot, though I'm reluctant to use the word *play* in conjunction with that doll's house, these days; it wasn't playing, or it was more than playing.

It was a big doll's house. One main house, as tall as I was at the age of seven, and two wings on either side. It was modelled on a Lübeck merchant house; my father had gone to a lot of trouble. Entrance hall, curved staircase, long gallery, first, second and third floors, kitchens and bathrooms, dining room, bedrooms, drawing room and library. There were fireplaces, grandfather clocks, bookcases, bureaus, a piano and tiny mirrors, velvet curtains, miniature chandeliers and a doorbell the size of a matchstick head on the double front door.

That was the outer appearance.

Behind it, a second doll's house was secreted away – a doll's house of hiding places. Trapdoors and concealed openings, wardrobes giving way to chambers, walls that swung open onto windowless cells. I have never asked my father what he was thinking when he built it. I suspect he wanted to hint at the existence of secrets. Rooms behind rooms. Double meanings: he wanted me to know that nothing was the way it seemed to be. Our family, like every family no doubt, had secrets. It still does. The doll's house, I think these days, was a practice ground.

In my dream I was lying awake in bed. My bedroom was dark but for the matte oval light cast through the glass pane in the door onto the wooden floor, far away from the room where my parents would sit together in the evening. I was wide awake and I saw an impish creature flitting across the low room. Humpbacked and soundless, it flitted from one spot to the next and lastly into the doll's house. I have always been more afraid of small creatures than of large ones. I called for my parents. I screamed for my parents; it took an eternity but eventually they came, turned on the light, laughed at my horror, lit up the doll's house and found nothing, of course, because the creature had crept into one of the hiding places. My father knew the hiding places were there. I knew the creature was there. But it was no use; my mother tucked me in tight and then they went out, leaving me alone to lie on my back, listening, staring at the outline of the doll's house as something evil contracted silently inside it. I knew there was something there which would come back, and that's the end of the dream; here is where dream and reality merge.

I'm sure there's some detail I've forgotten. That one tiny detail for which I dreamed the dream – while the fear, my thudding heart and inexplicable terror, are timeless, as if frozen in my memory.
What have I forgotten.

The doll's house had inhabitants. A family, a father and mother and several children, grandparents, aunts and uncles, dolls made of wood with woollen hair, felt shirts, their faces painted with round eyes, smiling mouths; I only ever really played with one of them, a girl with a red dress, brown boots and plaits: Anna. The other dolls were there, present, but I don't remember using them. The girl Anna was an emigrant within the family. An orphan who had to hide from something, and I did that whenever I played with her. I hid her.

These days, the doll's house is in the attic at the house by the sea. The main doll's house, that is; the side wings have disappeared, much of the furniture is lost, almost all the dolls are gone. The rooms are laid waste, the few remaining objects broken, a three-legged table, a little bed with its covers torn off, the pictures askew on the walls, the tiny mirrors shattered, the banisters snapped; a bomb has been dropped on the doll's house, a war has taken place. I don't know who left it that way; I've rarely seen children playing with it. All sorts of children were there, my own, Ada's children, other guests' children, my brother's and sister's children, but I never saw any of them playing with the doll's house the way I did as a child. I'm not judging – merely stating. Perhaps the doll's house has its own aura, a chalk circle. It has a magical ring round it that cannot be broken, and the other children see something different to what I saw as a child. I don't know whether my son or Ada's daughter discovered a concealed door, opened up an in-between space, came across one of the secret chambers; I never pointed the rooms out to any of the children. The doll's house's devastation didn't take place deliberately, it just happened. The doll's house was abandoned, like a real house, became a vacant house; one day a window was smashed and then another, and then small and larger creatures slipped into the house and spun webs, built nests. Birch trees sprouted out of the rafters, someone chopped up the furniture in the entrance hall and lit a fire, this material settled between the walls with the others, the shadows.

Gold, patina, darkness.

Something about it is right. The wooden clan, the friendly, simple-minded characters with their smiling faces, round heads, have scattered to the winds, losing arms and legs; their heads have rolled, torn-off feet and chopped-off hands in among the broken objects. Eyeballs. And it's truly the case that only Anna is left and that I come across her when I go to the house by the sea in search of the thread running through my writing, sit down by the doll's house and peer into its rooms:

The seventh little goat, hidden from the wolf.
Still there.

Leaning on the wall in a corner by a wardrobe, its doors torn off its hinges. Her felt dress and her brown plaits, her face darker than her arms; perhaps I used to hold her by her head, forty-five years ago. I took a photo of her in her corner behind the wardrobe, a phone photo that looked so ghostly – the room a crime scene, the chaos an act of violence – that I had to rescue her by picking her up with an astonishingly vehement motion and putting her in my pocket. At home I took her out and placed her on my desk. A day later, I went back to the summer house to fetch her one last intact little chair.

The chair is now to the left of my computer, with her sitting on it. She's not looking at me, she has her back turned to me. We're both looking out of the same window, both sitting on a chair, her motionless, me more or less motionless; there's a link between me and her. She's not a Russian doll – there are no smaller, even smaller and very last dolls hidden inside her – but of course there is something hidden inside her, and it's possible that all my female characters are tied to this wooden girl, all my stories started in the doll's house. My father built me a house, and he taught me to read as early as possible. I was four when I started reading and he therefore stopped reading to me before I started school at age six; in a way, there was nothing more for him to do for me, and in another way, that may have been the right thing, and enough.

Last year, my sister gave me a book from our childhood as a Christmas present. It was the second Christmas we didn't celebrate together, since the pandemic drove our family apart; my sister, who has two children and lives in France, didn't want to leave the country while Omicron was raging. I spent Christmas with my son and his father; my son unpacked my sister's Christmas parcel and at the very top of it was a book we had once talked about on the phone, during one of those long, melancholy lockdown calls.

The Yellow House. The German edition is no longer in print; a much-read tatty copy is available online for a hundred euros. The front cover, thick A4-sized cardboard, depicts a yellow apartment building with three floors and six windows. When you open it up you're inside the house. The stairwell on the left, and on the right six little books in three rows of two, six doors on their title pages, and behind them: the flats. Yellow walls, spherical lamps, blue-painted stairs, linoleum floors, an ornate sign next to the front door listing the names of the tenants – all this resembles the building where we grew up. I loved *The Yellow House* as a child. To open up its inner booklets was to open the door to a flat, to become an invisible intruder in another life. The concierge with his canary and cat on the ground floor, the music teacher in the attic, the peaceful family on the first floor. The most sinister, vibrating flat was the home of A. Oswald on the second floor, and it was sinister and vibrating because A. Oswald was not at home. When I opened up the door page, I found myself in a darkened hallway by an empty coat stand, and another door led from this hallway into an abandoned room where a tortoise came crawling out from behind a curtain.

Silence.

As my son extracted this book from his aunt's parcel that exceptional Christmas forty years later and passed it to me with a questioning, sceptical look, that precise feeling came straight back to me – tense expectation. I had the book on my lap, listening, and at the same time I found myself in A. Oswald's abandoned flat, listening – for something.

To open the door to the flat where I grew up was to step inside a secret. Impossible to bring other children home with me without notice; I couldn't just turn up with one or two friends like all the other children I knew (in the first six years of my life, I knew none). I did not grow up in an open house – which may be one reason why the Yellow House, that secret in the silent second-floor flat on the left, drew me in. Our house was a house of atmospheres, forebodings, states of mind; it was uncertain, unintelligible and, for a child, absolutely unpredictable.

I grew up with my grandmother, which you might call unconventional; perhaps that would be an innocuous word for our circumstances. We lived with my parents, the four of us in a large old flat in the West Berlin borough of Neukölln with many rooms, bright, half-bright and dark. Box rooms crammed with stuff, ceilings suspended for storage above, cardboard boxes full of papers, bookshelves pushed in front of double doors, stacks of books, corridors between book stacks. Nobody cleaned. Everything was dusty. Dirty plates gathered in the kitchen, old newspapers, empty bottles beside the front door, heaps of clothes by the washing machine, which my mother stuffed into the machine before taking off her coat when she came home from work; my mother earned the family's money. During the seven years when I was an only child, my father was studying mathematics and physics; he was depressive, perhaps that would be an innocuous term for his states of mind. My grandmother tried to keep an eye on everything. She supervised me, though she was no less depressive; she spent years in psychiatric hospitals and had suffered a severe case of polio at the age of fifty, been entirely paralysed and then recovered, but the left side of her body remained vulnerable and numb; she was handicapped, found it hard to be touched and resisted physical affection. I can't remember anyone laughing in our home. Or singing. Happiness, a simple, harmonious form of being together, a family outing, a contented supper, was inconceivable; we had to *ask God for forgiveness* for the word 'happiness'. Everything was fragile. Objects were packed in crates and boxes, obstructed, cupboards placed in front of other cupboards, the flat a reproduction of the doll's house, the doll's house the flat in miniature form.

My grandmother stood at the cooker making Russian bread soup. Soup made of stale breadcrusts with raisins and shrivelled apples. She was born in Petersburg, her mother tongue Russian. She had been brought to Germany on a sled during the revolution and sometimes wore a silver brooch modelled on a troika: a bearded coachman, a tiny sled pulled at great speed by three misshapen horses; I was allowed to look at the brooch as long as I liked but never to touch it. My grandmother had been brought on the sled to her grandparents, to the house by the sea. She stayed there for years; when her parents reappeared to fetch her to Berlin, the story went, she didn't recognize them and curtseyed to her mother. I knew these things about my grandmother as I sat at the kitchen table and watched her stirring the soup; she wore a crumpled embroidered apron that looked distinctly like a costume, an ironic citation. She was short and delicate, lean, her left arm always splayed unnaturally away from her body as though that half of her wanted to go elsewhere, in another direction, ultimately to a different place; her body was divided down the middle, my grandmother split into two halves. She wore thick glasses, the steam from the soup fogging her lenses as she turned blindly to face me. I don't know how I knew these things about my grandmother; we never spoke about them. What it had been like not to recognize her own mother. To lie inside a machine called an iron lung, to breathe inside that machine; I knew my grandmother had been in an iron lung with her polio; I never asked her about it. There were stories that were repeated mantra-like – Petersburg, my grandmother's grandfather, a lighthouse keeper, silverware from Tula, a cat-skin blanket swaddling my grandmother as she crossed the deep Russian snow. And there were the silent mantras, far louder, almost droning. War years, post-war years, questions of guilt and remorse, dark mechanics, patchworks of allusion, abyss, horror. My grandmother stirred the bread soup, cocked her head as if hearing something far away, as if apprehending a truth, then she said, without meaning me or anyone in particular: If you sing in the morning, the cat'll get you at night. The cat: 'die Katze'. Her way of pronouncing the word, the deep and precise satisfaction of it. She said: Pride. Comes. Before. A fall. She said: Spider in the morning brings you a warning, spider at night heralds delight. She made her bread soup for my father. My father wanted to eat bread soup, my father wanted to live in a war. He lived, though, in peacetime. In the strange, disordered peacetime of the 1970s, and when he was not writing numbers he sat in a green armchair with the curtains closed in broad daylight, listening to excruciatingly loud music that I recognized much later as Mozart's *Don Giovanni*, crying, and my grandmother could neither prevent him nor console him, nor could she explain that crying to me. Of course, I thought he was crying because of me. He was crying because something was wrong with me, because I was – lacking something. When he wasn't crying or working on his PhD or staring at his thesis – a motionless figure, brow heavy in his hands at a desk strewn with notes, crumpled-up notes around the desk, a wastepaper basket overflowing with notes and everywhere the diffuse blue smoke of cigarettes – he would break out in rages. The word 'temper' was used in our family like the words 'cold', 'hot', 'large', 'small': an adjective. Your father has a violent temper, my grandmother told me objectively. My father's temper descended out of the blue upon me, upon us. My father raged. He destroyed furniture, broke things, he shredded, kicked apart, ripped, he rampaged, he foamed at the mouth. Fits of anger. Once they were over, we all had to lie down. The world had been devastated, the devastated world was part of the actual world, and the actual world was simply rebuilt after a brief regeneration, restored over and over again. Respite to breathe. Light falling. My grandmother nestled the delicate, black-tarnished silver spoons from Tula back together, swept up the shards, swept the shards into the knocked-over boxes, piled the boxes on top of one another. Coughed. Touched her left shoulder with the edge of her right wrist. Put on her beret, clicked her thumb and middle finger above her head to ward off something floating there that I couldn't see, and left the house for a while. She bore part of the guilt for her son's circumstances; she shouldered that guilt, a troublesome shambles that I had somehow been drawn into. I don't know who I was for my father; I certainly wasn't his child. I was a grandchild – the grandchild of my grandmother, who had had three children; the middle one had taken his own life at the age of twenty, shortly before I was born. You were born into a house in mourning, my grandmother liked to say, pronouncing the words with the same satisfaction as the word 'Katze'. She also said: You're the light in our darkness, which confused me; no one acted as though I were a light. My grandmother's hands. Her brown, papery, liver-spotted skin, her slim fingers, which she sometimes bent pensively and placed on my cheek, a talon that was always cold. Her peculiar scent of pinewood, of soot and hot stones, ground roots. I loved my grandmother very much. She protected me, passively. She didn't try to explain things to me, she just let them happen; she must have thought it over and decided that was the only right thing to do. She tried to be with me; she could do no more than that. Her three children were born out of wedlock, all by the same man: my grandfather, that is. From time to time I was taken to visit him alone; I remember fearing and hating him. In his squalid single room, olive-coloured, coated in smoke and warmth, stood a home pool table, under which I immediately sat cross-legged, not coming out for the length of my visit. I always had a book with me and promptly opened it up, covered my ears and read until it was over and someone came to collect me, to deliver me from my grandfather. My grandfather smoked without pause, drank hard liquor, sat or lay on an unmade sofa bed behind a low table beneath a dusty wicker lampshade, a horrific wire monkey dangling from the wicker lampshade, books piled on the table, tattered manuscripts and opened sardine tins around a typewriter. Next to my grandfather sat a woman with narrow eyes and white hair down to her hips, in a coat of mangy leopard skin with wrists jangling with silver jewellery; she smoked through a meerschaum cigarette holder and watched me doggedly, not blinking. They listened to the music my father listened to and threw biscuits and bottle tops under the pool table as if I were a wild animal; perhaps I was. My grandfather never visited us. His youngest son come to visit us now and then, the only brother left to my father, whom he'd have gladly swapped, I knew, for his lost brother. Yet there was still a tie between them, which was evident because they would perform grotesque imitations of my grandmother, their mother. Her split gait, her manner of speaking, her superstitions and finger-clicking, her habit of murmuring isolated lines of poetry to herself and then listening into the void, as if the poems continued there. Her short-sightedness, angry nervousness, her division in two; when they were together they imitated their mother with an expression so utterly distraught, it was obvious even to a child. I loved the uncle I had left. I was certain I would have loved my dead uncle more, but I loved this one too. He was fifteen years older than me, already an impressive alcoholic by his mid-twenties, unemployed and of no fixed abode; he wore a hat with earflaps and a ripped sheepskin-lined leather jacket; he emanated fantastic self-assurance. My grandmother never stood up to her sons. It was excruciating for me to watch the spectacle of their imitation, but there was something about it that made me feel it might reveal something to me. A weakness of my father's. A way out for me. When his brother was around, my father was distracted from me; I understood that. I sensed a caesura in his otherwise incessant and ambivalent focus on me; barely perceptible, but nonetheless. It existed. My uncle would leave us late at night, and during the nights after his visits my father would sleepwalk, stand listening at the open front door until my mother led him back to bed, but in the morning he'd wake up beneath the scratched grand piano that had belonged to his father, pillow pressed to his face, and then he'd get up and heap coal into the tiled stoves.

What did he dream.

I never asked him.

Everything was there without us ever speaking about it. I can't remember anyone ever speaking, in any case. There was reading. Calculating. Ripping of paper. Someone playing the piano. My grandmother cracked nutmeg shells, ground up cacti, burned sage brush. She whispered Russian vocabulary and played Napoleon at St Helena, and when she won her game of patience she would knock on wood; if she lost she'd scrub the card table vigorously with ash. My father closed the curtains and cried and then he smashed crockery. Horrendous. My mother came home unfathomably late; sometimes I felt I had only imagined my mother, I had read about a mother in books. The doors to the closets were closed, opening them was forbidden. My father claimed we had a lodger, a stunted man who lived in the space above the suspended ceiling over the darkroom; sometimes the trapdoor to the suspended ceiling was ajar, a cork hanging down on a string, bay leaves and confetti scattered on the floorboards. Whoever lived above that ceiling could see through the gap and the oval glass window in my bedroom door, all the way to my bed. My father had a clear desire to frighten me.

When I was four my grandmother took me to the house by the sea where she had spent her childhood. Her aunt had died and my grandmother had inherited the house and the land overnight. The house was called Daheim, Home; my question about the reason for the name went unanswered. The ground floor was inhabited by ethnic German expellees, another word I had to accept without explanation, a family of four from Romania with whom we shared the garden and the outside toilet. My grandmother moved us into the upper floor: two rooms, between them a windowless corridor coated in spiders' webs and strewn with dead moths. She got hold of an electric kettle, packet tomato soup and tinned peaches, and we sat in that corridor, drank the tomato soup out of enamel mugs, spooned the peaches out of the tin and warmed our hands over a tea light.

Did we do it because we had to.

Or was that simply how my grandmother imagined an arrival, was she staging the world for me.

Crates and boxes, this house too, a place of crates and boxes, a trunk containing neat piles of mouldering centuries-old linens; my grandmother made me a first bed in that trunk before she cleared out the alcove in which I slept until I was ten. Her family had disowned her for her illegitimate children, not let her set foot in the house for forty years. It must have been strange to be back there so suddenly, with her grandchild, with her beautifully sad, tough life behind her. If there's a time when I'd have liked to have been my grandmother, it's during those first years of her return to the sea. She was sixty; so much was over, so much survived. She went bathing in the harbour, even in autumn and winter, and I was allowed to watch her bathing; I saw her naked, otherwise never; she was prudish and imperious in her prudishness. At night the expellees would sing in the kitchen, lament and throw glasses at the wall. I lay listening beneath my heavy eiderdown, my grandmother in bed, drinking sherry and reading Fontane by the dim ochre light of a clip lamp; she said: You go to sleep now. Go on. Sometimes we went to the phone box at the village square and called my parents. I remember the dial winding back on the grey telephone, the jangling coins in my hand, the weight of the receiver against my ear; I don't remember the conversations. On our way back to the city, four hundred miles, a long journey in those days, I cried and went on crying until we arrived; I was a histrionic child. My grandmother had nothing to say about my crying, as with all crying, apart from a single sentence: You know you can come back again.

She said: You know you can come back, a consolation I did not understand at the time. But now, at the age of fifty-two, I do understand it.
How long some things take to reach you.

The city – that was the complicated, obstructed, demented flat, its light as if underwater, rooms full of wilting crane flowers and lilies, the stairwell that smelled of wet linoleum, vinegar and coal, a heavy felt curtain inside the door, the mysterious copper-red light falling through the pane into the hall, and I sat behind the felt curtain and waited, embittered, for my mother to come home. The city was the puppet theatre my father had built for me after the doll's house. Tall and bulky, made of green-varnished wood with a red gable on which a cat played a violin, teeth bared; my father had painted magnificent backdrops, made puppets. He and my mother disappeared behind the theatre and put on *Jorinde and Joringel*, *Rapunzel* and *Bluebeard*, mainly *Bluebeard* over and over. The backdrop of the room with the beheaded wives was spectacular, headless torsos dangling from the ceiling on meat hooks, but the witches were just as spectacular, their red fired-clay heads, hooked noses, their black-tangled hair and their horribly sky-blue eyes. I begged my mother to come out from behind the theatre. My mother, on my father's instructions, claimed she wasn't behind the theatre so she couldn't come out. It was intractable, I had to put my own hands over my eyes. That was the city – my father in his armchair with the music and his fist clenched against his temple, a position I rediscovered in my grandfather, but for my grandfather it was derisive; with my father, appalling. I knew that my grandfather, as absent as he was, ruled over the family and was one cause of its misery; when he died I was seven and far from sad about his death.

My father took me along to his father's laying out. I didn't know where we were going; my father had decided to confront me with the sight of my dead grandfather on a pedestal in a cold chapel without preparing me for it. My father had several noticeable scratches on his hands, and when I asked him about them he said they came from the cat I'd been given for Christmas a few weeks previously, a cuddly toy with black and white fur and jade-green eyes, which I'd been carrying around with me uninterrupted since Christmas. I didn't understand how it could have scratched him, and he said its fur was real and that meant the whole cat was real, or at least had once been real. He said that, like everything that had once lived, this cat still had certain reflexes after death, after being turned into a cuddly toy, and those reflexes had made it scratch and fight, like a chicken running headless around a farmyard. He didn't take it back. He didn't say, Sorry, that's nonsense of course. He let it stand, and as I remember our journey to my grandfather's laying out, I might think my father had wanted something to fracture the shock ahead of us; he did want to prepare me, in exactly the outlandish and crazy way he ultimately prepared me for almost everything. He could have told me a story about himself and his father. And he didn't do that, or he did it indirectly, which I obviously didn't understand as a child. He thought up a story that neatly skirted what happened, a story exactly tangential to the truth. An ugly story and yet, or for that very reason: he had an intention, just less to do with me and more to do with him and his dead father. And I spot something of that egocentric intention in myself when I think of the moment I begin writing a story – an almost complete aloneness.

I didn't think that at the time, though, of course. Standing before my laid-out, finally dead grandfather, I looked at the scratches on my father's hands; I never touched that black and white cat again, it was ruined for me, the smell of my grandfather's corpse passed over to it.

My mother. My mother was not in charge of outings of this kind. Hard to say what she was in charge of. She earned the family's money, that's what she was in charge of, and my father spent it – on cigarettes, books and battered furniture, which he picked up from the junk shops on Sonnenallee and used to barricade the rooms. By the time I got up in the morning, my mother had long since left the house and she didn't come back until the evening, loaded down with shopping for us, always with flowers, near-faded roses, dahlias, fuchsias from the florist's where she had worked since she was sixteen. My mother was a distinctly beautiful woman. She wore that beauty to the flower shop and then she wore it home again. My father often photographed her with a Rolleiflex, a twin-eyed reflex camera into which he stared, as I saw it, as if into an abyss, always away from the person he was photographing; she would pose in positions that seem to me now like the opposite of her nature, but who knows – I've only experienced my mother as my mother. There was a darkroom set up in one of the flat's closets; when my father was well enough he and I would develop his photos together. I stood beside him in that cramped space, in the red light of the darkroom lamp, and watched my mother's face appearing on the photo paper in the liquid inside the plastic tray, always black and white, challenging and enigmatic, beautiful, a total stranger. My father came up with scripts for short films, which he made on his Super-8 camera; my mother had to swallow flower petals and lift up the lids of soup tureens seething with woodlice; she was to lie down in the trunk in the house by the sea as if the trunk were a coffin, and she did it.

She did that.

But I suspect her mind was elsewhere.

She never smoked her cigarettes in the flat, only ever on the balcony, and she smoked turned away from us all, apart and so disconnected that no one ever joined her. She decorated the stairwell with lush pink and yellow gladioli, she wore a jacket of light-sparking rabbit skin, she wore lipstick, and on days like the one when I went with my father to my grandfather's laying out, we'd find Joan Baez on the record player when we got back. My mother could be literally carefree. She listened to Donovan. Cat Stevens. Bob Dylan. She did it when she was apart from us; she had, like everyone it seems, her own life, her secret and despite it all sometimes happy life, and perhaps she was in charge of letting me know exactly that. Her mother had tried in vain to stop my parents from marrying. She had gone to visit my father's mother and asked her to keep her nightmare of a son from ruining her daughter's life; her plea was not heard. My mother must have been obsessed with leaving her circumstances behind her. Her circumstances were the opposite of my father's; perhaps my mother had only been aware of the difference, not the calamity. Or she had been aware of the calamity and she dared to face it. Rightly so.

My maternal grandmother was heavy, short of breath, plagued by gout; she rarely left her flat, sat instead on her balcony and watched the world go by beyond parapet and lavender. She smoked

Lux-brand cigarettes, drank beer out of cans washed down with brandy; she came from the working-class Wedding district, had sold flowers in the high-end Kaufhaus des Westens department store. She didn't read books. She read the tabloids. She was an excellent cook. She sang songs. She said: Laugh at life and it'll laugh right back – if you laugh at it; only that *if* seemed to hint at any possible difficulties. She was rarely ambiguous, unable to comprehend my other grandmother's bizarre Russian superstitions. She was affectionate, tender in a direct way, she wanted to be hugged and kissed, and she wanted to hug me and would kiss me vigorously. But in one of my recurring childhood dreams I was climbing the stairs to her flat with her, which was laborious and slow; she was lumbering, in pain, managed three steps and then had to rest; in those days there was a chair on every landing, not just in her building. In my dream, I knew we had not much time left to get into her flat, to reach safety; I knew that somewhere in a distant room a clock meant for us would first chime and then fall silent, and when the clock stopped chiming the stairwell would fall apart. The walls would glow, change colour and consistency, start melting, dissolving, and we would be lost. And in every dream, my grandmother didn't know that.

She was entirely immersed in her climbing, her footsteps and pauses for breath, she couldn't be hurried, she couldn't go faster. Always, that clock chimed – far away, on the edge of a circle of light and unalterable. Fell silent. The walls began to phosphoresce, the floor to sway. My heart thudded, then I woke up. This grandmother was alone in a different way to my father's mother. She had three strong, healthy children, and by the end of her life seven grandchildren, but she was alone. She died alone. Once I started school I was allowed to go to her place for lunch at the end of the short school day, a protective space before I had to go home. She cooked the food I liked, unlike my father, who deliberately cooked things I didn't want to eat. She said: You don't have to eat up. She sat on a bench by the cooker, her gouty hands folded in her lap, and watched me eat.

Potatoes boiled in their skins and peeled on the plate.
White cheese.
Yellow oil.
My grandmother loved watching me eat.

She didn't pepper me with questions. She was afraid of my father but she never asked me to betray him; she came to her own conclusions. When the TV series *Holocaust* aired in Germany in 1979 he and I went over to my grandmother's place. We didn't have a television set. She had one; the obligation to watch it must have been stronger than the disdain between them, they must have reached an agreement. The three of us sat on the settee, me in the middle. My father cried, his body wracked by sobs. My crying father was more familiar to me than my not-crying father. My grandmother sat on my right, popping beer cans open, smoking and watching him out of the corner of her eye and over my head; she thought her own thing. I leaned up against her. These days I know that her children's father, whom she'd divorced in the 1950s, was in the SS Death's Head Division. He died when my mother turned eighteen; his SS membership was revealed to her when she spotted the tattoo on the inside of his upper-left arm, on his deathbed. I sometimes think back to those evenings in my grandmother's lounge: three generations, two wars and total silence; we left immediately after the end of the programme. We left as the credits were rolling, and the thought of my grandmother, left behind in front of the television, abandoned to her thoughts, memories and the TV images, fills me with grief and helplessness. And also with terror.

Perhaps a fundamental image of childhood – growing into riddles. Hints and insinuations like towpaths, furtive secrets. The mysterious world of the grown-ups, their inscrutable behaviour, their unpredictable states of mind. Your own world, confined and yet unbounded, the appearance of structures like the first washed-out grey of dawn, the gradual understanding of patterns, dependencies. Every world is ambiguous. The coalman at the end of the road in a room below the earth, the word 'souterrain', and him sat behind a heap of silver-black egg-shaped briquettes, exposing himself, his erect member black with coal dust, the glans glowing red, a coral. The acoustics of our interlocking backyards. The warmth of the attic, where old women washed laundry in steaming cauldrons. Organ grinders with monkeys on chains. Knife sharpeners going from door to door. Divided Berlin, Sunday walks to the canal and the viewing towers from which my grandmother and I looked over to the East. The other city was foggy and lifeless, not a soul on the streets, windows boarded up, images from dreams, sooty smoke-taste of winter. The U-Bahn ran beneath this abandoned city, through ghost stations in which an unholy brown light glimmered, platforms strewn with rubble, soldiers with machine guns leaning motionless against shattered pillars. The U-Bahn ran so slowly it seemed almost to stand still; we trundled in slow-motion through a halted silence. We took this U-Bahn to Zehlendorf to walk in the forest and to view the house on the way to the forest where my father had grown up and grown sad, and which he and his brothers had sold when my grandmother went into the psychiatric hospital. A house in which strangers now lived, and my father told a story – he told it to no one, speaking to himself – of how he and his late brother cleared out the furniture and took it to the dump, of how a lorry with an open back had parked outside the house and they'd thrown each thing onto it separately. Not packed the things in boxes. Their mother's dresses on their hangers, plates, books, pictures. I believed his story – but then again, our entire flat was crammed full of books, plates, pictures, mirrors, silverware, the grand piano, the green sofa; where did it all come from, then.

There were no certainties.

My father built a hut in the snow, in the Zehlendorf forest, for the doll's house family. For the doll's house family outing, a charming shelter made of sticks and little branches with little mossy beds, the walls lined with fern to keep out the snow and the wind. A pebble path. A stable and a well.

Then he left me alone to play by myself. I went on an outing alone. The wooden Anna in a shelter in the undergrowth, on her bed of moss in her red dress and brown boots.

In a hiding place.
A partisan.

I remember all that, and at the same time I don't remember. No detailed sequence of events – then I did this, was that, gradually became this – none of all that. Stretches of black, soundless, an abrupt instant like a snapshot, back into something mute, something deaf. My brother and sister were born when I was seven, twins. I got to keep my big room with its corner window, but I vacated it by moving behind the puppet theatre. I occupied the theatre, setting up my own hiding place, the kind I knew from books. A narrow bed, a little table for candles, water, apples, dry bread, underneath the bed a menagerie of treasures and dust. Cherished pebbles, bread knives, banned books. The backdrops vanished, the witches too. The twins were dreamy, spent a lot of time drawing and sleeping, their fine hair always tangled at the back into delicate, gossamer-like nests. They went out in the hall at night in their small, misbuttoned pyjamas and called for our mother, they called: We've got needles in our eyes. There are needles in our eyes.

There was nothing anyone could do to stop them, they went on calling it over and over.

I'd like to say – that's enough now. This honourable invitation to a creative writing lectureship is not an interrogation, though I do feel it is one in a way: I'm interrogating myself. My writing is tied to those early years. Impressions, sensations, thoughts, intuitions from back then. Tied to the constitution of my family, a structure for which I will not give reasons. When I was twenty-five, I sat at a long table at Berlin's Literary Colloquium with nine other workshop participants and read out my short story 'The Red Coral Bracelet', the very first story I wrote. I had written it in Wewelsfleth, in Günter Grass's house, during a writers' residency one frosty and snowy January, far away from what I knew, far away from home. A moonstruck first-person narrator trying to untangle the knotted threads of her ancestors' lives, who leaves her lover, starts therapy and then bails out of it. *Is that the story I want to tell* – that line is a refrain, and I wrote it down without really thinking it through. I did feel it, though – and I think that it holds for everything I write. Now, more than twenty-five years later, I can see that the question of whether that is the story I wanted to tell genuinely is the central question. It touches on what made me, and it impresses me in an impersonal way that this was the first question I wrote down. In the workshop, the other participants wanted to hear about autobiographical aspects – did you have a Russian grandmother, a coral bracelet. I began to answer, eager to please, and it was the writer Katja Lange-Müller who cut me off, almost put her hand over my mouth.

She said: Now listen. You keep that to yourself, make sure of it.

And I kept it to myself. I've kept it to myself more or less to this day, and here too: kept to myself.

One of the reviewers of *Where Love Begins* wrote that I had two problems: I couldn't write and I had nothing to tell. Leaving the former aside, the latter comment has a peculiar truth to it. I do have nothing to tell, because what I actually have to tell, I can't tell. I can answer my question from the 'Red Coral Bracelet' story: No. No story is the one I wanted or needed to tell, not that or any other. But I *can* write about how I can't tell the actual story; the omission of the actual story pervades all my writing, and it has long since turned away from my family to face outwards, an act of transference, certainly in the psychoanalytical sense.

The family is not the only monstrous thing that happens to you. In the end, everything is monstrous. The actual story, the heart of the material, is not tellable per se; the centre is an inaccessible place. Telling stories, as that reviewer of *Where Love Begins* sees it, perhaps means making something up. But for me, making something up would mean wanting to leave reality and enter into a different reality – and that is precisely what I don't want. I want to enter into this one ungraspable reality, I want to write that I can't grasp it, and I want to insist that it is impossible, altogether unfeasible to grasp it.

When my son was little we'd often go to the puppet theatre. The coincidence of the puppet theatre of my childhood and this puppet theatre in Prenzlauer Berg genuinely only occurs to me now; likewise, the difference between the situations is only clear to me now. My son and I went to the puppet theatre on Dunckerstrasse, housed in a small ground-floor flat. Cloakroom and box office in the former kitchen, freshly baked waffles dusted with icing sugar, in winter mulled wine for the grown-ups and rosehip tea for the children; the flat was heated by a large tiled coal stove in one corner, it smelled musty and never got properly warm. Space for twenty in the audience, though we were often the only people at the afternoon performances, or sometimes there might be half a dozen of us. The programme changed, the puppeteers too, all of them no doubt from the East, trained in the large state-funded puppet theatres in Wismar and Erfurt, and they put on the best fairy tales: *Mother Hulda*, *Hansel and Gretel* and *Red Riding Hood*, and there was one puppeteer who performed the story of the three little pigs and the big bad wolf with a Russian accent. My son was an enthusiastic puppet theatregoer, wanted to go as often as possible. He'd answer Yeeeees!! when he was asked whether he was out there, he'd get very involved in the play, he'd laugh like crazy when it was funny, be upset when things turned serious; when he was scared he'd climb onto my lap and slip back onto his chair once the witch ended up in the oven. He showed that same heartfelt involvement with all fairy tales, but the one he loved most was the story of the three little pigs and the big bad wolf. It was because of the story, the puppeteer's voice – and perhaps because he was visible. The other players worked behind a wooden theatre arch like I'd had in my childhood bedroom; they acted while hidden, their hands concealed inside the puppets, their bodies not visible. The Russian puppeteer stood behind a table, his backdrop set up on a square of black felt. House, tree, fence, world – he wore a black polo neck, black trousers, he stood in front of a night-black wall, his puppets were marionettes, his hands danced and floated across the set, his face was white. Someone telling a story, but he didn't just tell it; he passed it on to the pigs and the wolf, stepping back behind the story and standing, at the same time, between it and the world.

What did I think of as my son and I sat in the second row of that darkened room in the dim warmth of the coal stove, usually in winter, and as we left into evening outside, the day over, and we'd go to the supermarket on Helmholtzplatz for frozen pizza and chocolate pudding, and then we'd go home; we'd watch the wolf demolishing the house of straw, the house of sticks, and I never once thought of

Bluebeard's chamber, the terrifying witch with her bristle-black hair and sky-blue eyes, of my puppet theatre, or of my father.

Now I think of all that.

Back then, with a child on my lap and cocooned in the present, I was protected and safe. It's strange that that protection no longer works, looking back.

When I turned sixteen, my father turned away from the family. He was exhausted; something was done with, had become immutable. He stopped watching us, watching me. I turned into thin air.

I took a breath of air.

In the summer of 1990 my grandmothers died, unexpectedly and one after another, and my father was committed to Neukölln Hospital's closed psychiatric ward and stayed there for five years, then moved to an open psychiatric unit and returned home in 2000, the year my son was born, returned to more or less normal life. I wrote a very short story about my father in my collection *Letti Park*, in which everything is said, literally, as far as I'm concerned. The story is called 'Poems' – a first-person narrator who visits her father, shares a piece of plum cake with him, remembering during her visit the years he spent on the psychiatric ward, and leaves again.

I could mention, with regard to the story, that it's closely linked for me to William Carlos Williams's poem about the plums in the icebox – I love that poem. I could mention that my grandmother naturally also belongs to the story, her habit of ambling around her garden in the grey dawn, between the redcurrant bushes and plum trees, of stopping abruptly, looking up at the sky, raising her forefinger and whispering: *Something from the mist-drenched air detached itself and grew overnight into a white shadow that clung around silver fir, tree and bush.** For years I thought those lines were a rather odd nursery rhyme, and it was a shock to find them, long after my grandmother's death, in Gottfried Benn's poem 'Hoar Frost'. Berlin's Kantstrasse also belongs to the story, where my parents now live in a very small annexe flat, the warmth of a late afternoon in August, the signal of the closing S-Bahn train doors at Savignyplatz Station, the balcony where I sit with my mother and watch her smoking while my father lays the coffee table for us with trembling hands. Obviously, in so-called reality he doesn't live alone in a flat crammed with boxes and crates, but

---

* From Gottfried Benn's poem 'Hoar Frost', translated by Martin Travers: https://gottfriedbennpoems.com/the-poems/

he is alone and the boxes, crates, death masks, the cat-skin blanket and the Tula silverware have been left behind in that old flat in Neukölln in a world now lost, though the fact that this world is now lost does not mean it has vanished; not at all. All that is there, it is connected and it was connected, and if I manage to be unobserved for a moment in my parents' small flat I can take it in my hands when I open the glass cabinet containing the crockery. The cabinet belonged to my grandmother. She kept her talismans inside it, her fossils, seashells, amber necklaces, Russian icons and voodoo dolls, her photo albums, copper rings and straw stars, and to this day – my grandmother has been dead for more than thirty years – I find her scent in that cabinet. I open the glass doors, stick my head inside, and there she is – ambergris, sage, sandalwood. Smoke.

Impossible to grasp.

Her voice, the way she laid her hand on the table as if on show, only ever her right hand, the left remaining on her lap; I see her, I can see how she was.

She does not appear in the story, but she does belong to the story, as do the years in which I visited my father on the closed psychiatric ward, years in which we were closer than ever before, and never as close again. Supper. He pushed the plastic tray with its separate sections for cold meat and cheese between himself and me, fending off all the others, the madmen who wanted something from me that was impossible to understand; he wiped the spray of their saliva casually off the table, fended off their stammers, their burning stares, their asserting and their touching, and laid a slice of mortadella on a slice of dry bread just for me.

Did he do that?

Or did I make it up.

I didn't make up that I read him poems, during those years. There were poems that moved him to tears, which is not necessarily linked to being in a mental hospital; anyone can and should have been moved to tears by a poem, at least once in their life. I insist on this story, I insist on all the things I'm not telling in it. The story is, to paraphrase John Burnside, liquid to my mind and my comprehension.

In Wewelsfleth I had a six-month residency from January into June. I had arrived in the middle of the night, the village pitch-dark, the fields around it inky-black, the front door of the Grass House wide open; I wanted to turn round and go straight back to Berlin. But then it began to snow, and the next morning the land outside the windows was white, and I stayed. There were two other residents who had tacitly agreed to leave each other alone, and I wanted to be left alone as well, to be alone in my beautiful rooms on the first floor with a view of the graveyard and the church and to find out whether I could write something and whether I wanted to, and if so, what.

I began the 'Red Coral Bracelet' story with a slight sense of doubt, uncertain whether it was permissible to tell a kitschy Russian fairy tale, and then I didn't care, and that was the beginning. I read about stove construction and nineteenth-century Petersburg in the Brockhaus Encyclopaedia on the bookshelves, I wrote in the mornings until after noon, I took a nap on a blue sofa and went for walks along the Elbe later in the day. The Elbe froze over. The world turned inside out. My Berlin friends sent theatre listings for the Volksbühne, with crosses by the premieres and *party* scrawled alongside, and I pinned up the listings above my desk for a while, and then I stopped. But I wrote about the Volksbühne, I wrote the story 'Bali Woman' and I made it snow, because it was snowing outside my windows and because those years were black and white, all years were, those of my childhood and teenage life too. I was at a distance from all that, a distance I'd never had before. At a distance from my family, my chosen family, my dead grandmothers, the city where I was born and grew up, from Ward Eighty-seven, where my father was wrestling demons, and for the very first time in my life I was alone. I talked to myself and to nobody else. I missed my friends, and at the same time I knew I had nothing to do with those friends, and I wrote the story 'The Summer House, Later'. Stein's outsiderhood was my own and the frozen lakes were the frozen Elbe, the yearning for things I did not possess positioning everything in sharp focus before me. Once, my father called from the ward and I whispered two paragraphs to him over the telephone affixed to the kitchen wall by the cooker, while the madmen seemed to be banging pots and pans and screaming in the background. He said: What a catastrophe, forget writing, and I said: Never call me again. Don't ever call me again, not once. I knew writing belonged to me. I'd understood it with an animal's instinct – it was mine. And I knew too that it evidently separated me from everything, that it isolated me. But I was content with that isolation, and I still am, with some reservations, to this day.

I was in my early thirties when my parents left the street where I grew up. My mother was sixty; she had spent her life on that street. Over the previous few years, my parents had come to be the only tenants left in the building and then in the entire block; an investor had bought up a whole stretch of the road and then let it run down, left flats vacant as people moved out; my parents stayed put. For three years, they were the last tenants in a complex made up of a front building, a side annexe and a rear building; forty flats, thirty-nine of them empty. The doors open, abandoned furniture smashed, tiled stoves removed, double-doors ripped out, brass handles screwed off, parquet broken out of the floors. The cellars housed mosquito colonies that swarmed in the spring, darkening the sky above the yard. The bins were no longer emptied, the pipes burst, water rose in the ground-floor flats, birches took root in the guttering. That was in 2003 in Berlin, but it was actually somewhere else, a void in time; time turned backwards in that building, warped, cancelled itself out. When I stood in the wet stairwell, still retaining its scent of damp mop, vinegar and coal, the building was how I'd always wished it could be as a child: empty, and I was invisible, and life was a possibility I could decide on or drop. I was standing inside the Yellow House, in my own childhood book, only eerier. I could push open the doors on the ground floor, on the third and fourth floors, and walk into the flats and there was no one there – but those who had been there had left traces of their energy, their shadows. The Yellow House was black. Only on the right-hand side of the second floor did something flash behind the copper-red glass pane in the door, and my mother drew aside the felt curtain rattling on its rod, opened the door and embraced me. In those winters the flat was so cold that my parents sat together in winter coats with hats on their heads and hot-water bottles on their laps, despite my father fuelling the stoves like a steamship stoker; in the summers they slept beneath mosquito nets as if in the tropics. They negotiated the rent down to a symbolic sum but that put them at the mercy of the situation, with all the things that weren't working; a fairy-tale position, which vitalized my father and caused my mother visible suffering. But then two new names appeared from one day to the next on the doorbell panel and the corresponding front doors, a third a week later.

Kazantzakis
  Mansfield

Bang

Someone planted catmint on a first-floor balcony and lights went on in the right-hand flat on the fourth floor, only turning off late at night. The same phenomenon in the building where my grandmother had lived, and a dim lamp glimmered out after dusk from the top floor of the last house on the street. My mother was confused but at the same time hopeful. She had the impression the flats were being rented out again after all; at least two new tenants had moved into the building, there somehow even though she never set eyes on them. That was what she wished for – her old street back, the street where she'd been a child, a simple street with cobbles and plane trees, a neglected park, ground-floor flats, backyards linking the buildings where everyday life took place; my mother knew that was something that definitely existed, elsewhere.

Kazantzakis, Mansfield, Bang.

I read the names by the doorbells, written in three different hands on three different tiny signs. I looked up at the blossoming catmint, at the paper stars hanging in the window. I knew my father had put up the name signs, planted the mint and presumably installed various lamps on a timer switch, and it took my mother a few weeks, but then she got it too. My father claimed he came up with it because he'd felt uncomfortable, he'd wanted to pretend other people were still living on their desolate street. Then he admitted to putting on the pretence for my mother's sake; he wanted her to feel safer. But ultimately he had come up with it for himself, a game that entertained and amused him; had my mother fallen for it for longer, he'd have gone to more trouble. He'd have played music, pegged up laundry in the yard and accepted parcels for Kazantzakis. For my father, those years in the empty house were happy years; the house in its ravaged abandonment was a perfect match for his attitude to life, he had become one with the world there after all, and if it had been up to him it would have stayed that way to the end. But at some point my mother could no longer stand it, and after the third winter we children intervened, got our way, and they moved out. They moved from four bedrooms in Neukölln to their one-bedroom backyard flat in urbane Charlottenburg, my mother puffed up with pride at their new address and yet broken-hearted. They took the books and some of the battered furniture to the house by the sea. The puppet theatre must have got lost in the move, the wide wings of the doll's house, the darkroom equipment, the records and desks, the green armchair and the midget lodger as well. They left the grand piano where it was and it was up to me to take care of it, my father's living legacy to me. When I arrived at the flat one last time to remove it, the place was empty other than the piano. The doors between the rooms were wide open for the very first time, sun falling upon the parquet. Bundles of light brimming with dust, decades' worth of particles. Silence. In the bay window hung one last little message, pinned to the wall: *We are such stuff as dreams are made on and our little life is rounded with a sleep.* I was standing on the balcony smoking as the piano removers came down the street, an enormous truck with a picture of a fire-breathing dragon, a coincidence. Two tattooed giants lugged the grand piano down the stairs, manoeuvred it into the truck, took it away; they heaved it into the dragon's maws and vanished.

I stayed behind in the flat, walking again through the empty rooms, but there was no gesture and no line that might have matched how I felt – if I felt anything at all; I felt, I believe, nothing.

Then I closed the front door behind me.

Self and pity. Every description, every report is a deceptive ordering of reality, of images and splinters, of dreams. When I turned thirty I became a mother, and in the first summer with my baby we went to the coast, to my grandmother's house where I had not been since her death, not been for years. My uncle had set himself up in the room below the stairs and our appearance fetched him back from a sleep, from an almost spaced-out daydream; he rubbed his eyes: other people.

The rest of the house was unchanged – a dusty, spider-inhabited museum. In the wardrobes my grandmother's dresses, her books on the bedside table, bookmarks between the pages, her magnifying glass, her copper bracelets, patience cards, fuller's earth capsules, her water glass. The furniture from the Neukölln flat crammed into the barn, including the cot the twins and I had slept in, and I heaved it out, cleaned it up, put on fresh sheets, laid my own child in it and stared in amazement. In those first years, the house belonged to me. My uncle submitted gracefully to this invasion of reality, letting me do whatever I liked. My father had been discharged from the psychiatric ward but he was weak, my mother by his side; my sister was studying in Paris, my brother serving in the Bundeswehr; I had the house, I had the world to myself. I opened all the windows, swept the rooms, took my grandmother's dresses to the Salvation Army. And then I invited my Berlin friends over – I did what I'd never have done as a child, I opened the door wide and let them all in. I brought, as Ada later explained, my own, my chosen family into the family house.

Just as Ada never detailed the reasons for her split from her parents to me, I did not explain mine to her. She knew there was something not right – the house was too chaotic, the interior too pathological, my uncle too crazy, the garden too overgrown, and all of it open, nothing out of bounds, no one's rules to follow; we did whatever we liked and everyone came by. Someone or other, Ada understood, had had a screw loose, someone had hanged himself and someone else had lost their mind entirely, and it was clear that a disempowerment had taken place, a palace coup; it might have been dangerous to ask why.

All in all, this family I'd chosen for myself displayed a surprisingly familiar lack of words and language. It was not usual to tell each other things, to ask someone a serious question, wait for the answer, listen and consider, to ask a new question or add something of one's own – in a way, there was constant talking and in another way none at all. It was a wild togetherness. Affectionate, tender, built on big emotions, warmth and yearning, those years seemed to come as close as ever possible to a family. But had one of us had to say of another where they actually came from, where they'd been before, we'd all have had to pass. My uncle was the only one who occasionally reached for the musty root that came up time and again in his autobiographical edifice, a rusted barb: he wanted to say something about his mother. About my father. His dead brother, something about the reason for the state of the house, the actual causes of our togetherness. Whenever he started, usually late at night after a whole lot of alcohol, I'd get up and go to bed. Without me he didn't want to talk about it, so he'd break off, and no one asked him any questions. Present – we wanted a permanent present day, as much of it as possible, before things were pulled out from under our feet again through whatever subversions came along, ripped out of our hands. The adults drank and smoked like crazy. The children were autonomous, benignly neglected, unkempt and barefoot; they never had to go to bed, falling asleep on their feet in the last hours of the day, and someone would catch their fall and put them down in a random bed. Sleep was an absence. It was incomprehensibly moving to see the others at long last at noon, having only parted at daybreak. Ada and I were the first in the kitchen, and the two of us cleared away the empty glasses and bottles, bought bread rolls, smoked fish and melons, and laid the table for breakfast; we sat at the table with the children, our own and the others', and watched devotedly as they ate Choco Pops and drank cocoa; we had no need to speak about what it meant to us. That silence was the price to be paid for this kind of togetherness, and I think that's fine, even if it means we've all lost touch now, with a few exceptions.

During those years I wrote my second book, *Nothing but Ghosts*. I sat among the others on the patio at a wobbly side table with tea and, back then, huge amounts of cigarettes, and I wrote one or two pages of a story as that specific choreography unfolded around me, the mocking way of wishing each other good morning at noon, the chairs that circled the house with the sun, who wants another coffee, I might just have a little glass of ice-cold Vinho Verde, the sound the children's bare feet made on the flagstones when they ran, their fast-flying breathing and their conspiratorial laughter; I could see Ada taking the washing down from the line and I rarely thought her as beautiful as in those motions – on tiptoe, her stretched arms, the meticulous folding of sheets, shaking of beach towels, the way she bent to take the pegs out of the basket, the way she was immersed. I started a third page, then I got up and went to see what was on the shopping list on the kitchen windowsill, where everyone wrote down what they wanted and everyone got what they wanted. I'd read Carson McCullers' *The Member of the Wedding*, that scene where Frankie is sitting in the kitchen with her cousin John Henry and the Black cook Berenice while a piano's being tuned in the neighbourhood. It's oppressively hot, a storm brewing, John Henry sitting on Berenice's lap, and then Frankie sits on Berenice's lap too, and they talk about love while the piano tuner's ccc aaa rings out to them from a nearby house. The incomplete scale, the unresolved seventh chord, the whole scene is so full of virtually ecstatic unstilled yearning, of craving, apprehension, grief; I couldn't remember ever having read anything as wonderful and perfect. I wanted to have something of that in my stories – the break-off of closeness, the hurt, the sorrow and the beauty of it all. In Jim Jarmusch's *Down by Law* there's the farewell between Zack and Jack, the end of the film, road movie over, and the three protagonists are about to part ways, have already parted ways. John Lurie and Tom Waits are standing at a fork in the road, Waits holds out his hand to bid Lurie farewell – and draws it back again. And takes the right-hand path while Lurie takes the left. And that's it.

That's it.

My emotional reaction to reading *The Member of the Wedding* was similarly extreme to my indignation over the end of the film, a shocked disbelief; I remember leaving the cinema as if under anaesthetic. I knew Jarmusch was right, that that was how we all have to part ways, the only option for survival. Don't touch me – I wanted the people in my stories to speak that language, to talk past one another, with exactly the precision and cruelty we summon up when we love the other person. When we love so hard we want to stop breathing. Die. Break into pieces. The shopping list said *beer, vodka, wine, cigarettes, fish* and *lemons*, and someone had added *night, mosquitoes* and *ignorance*, and out of the crypt of his bedroom my uncle surfaced with his face shattered by too little sleep and too much alcohol, his flies undone; he was the bond that reminded me both blurrily and reliably of my family – something I could live with. Ada walked to the village barefoot, the children straggling after her. I shut my computer. Later I opened it again to place a word in the text, like a cross-stitch, a margin. Glamouring. Everything was sad and illuminated and no one asked me what I was doing, what I was writing and what about.

Would I have wanted to be asked?
No.

When the summers were over and one after another went back to Berlin, we hugged goodbye. It wasn't like in *Down by Law*. We hugged and kissed, and we cried, and the children were very interested in that type of tears. They'd stand with their little heads cocked and watch us from below, and when they saw we were crying they were contented and calm – they'd done everything right. In the drawing room, the space where the house's museum of furniture had reached its highest density – Sunday dinner service in the glass cabinet, grandfather clock, Biedermeier sofa and certificates from Russia's Patriotic Wars – a gold-framed photograph of my great-great-grandparents' golden wedding hung above the piano. A spring day in 1927, the two of them seated beneath still-bare trees in front of the house amid their family, neighbours and friends. Without consciously thinking of the photo, I imitated it – on the last day of summer, we'd gather outside the house and wait for a stranger we could ask to photograph us, and at some point someone would pass by and do it for us. Sometimes the classic, standing together, the children down on the grass; for another photo we lined up by height, my son the very smallest and my uncle the oldest and tallest. There were group photos with many and few people, in sunshine and pouring rain, and in all the photos we could see the children growing and getting older, a flip-book of time; in the last photos the children are almost leaping out of the pictures, still there, then they're gone – they're gone.

Ada, Ronald, Robert, Michael, Stein, Marco, Peter and Torsten, Vince, Paulina, Lotti, Paul and Martin and Franz and me. August 2004, at the end of a glowing, hot summer. How we must have looked through the eyes of the stranger photographing us – happy wild things. I'd get the photos developed at the supermarket and wedge them between the glass and the wood of the kitchen cupboard. It would never have occurred to me to frame them, though they were more important to me at the time than anything else I possessed.

Many years later – once those summers were over, once I had started my analysis, given up smoking, written my third book, *Alice*, in the early hours of the morning in an always identical, precisely timed procedure at my kitchen table in Berlin, a discipline and a punishment – I dreamed an unexpected series of recurring dreams of a missed summer. In each dream, the summer was over and I was packing my case in my attic room at the house. I folded my summer dresses, packed the unread books, put my sandals away under the wardrobe, and as I did so it occurred to me that I hadn't been swimming this year. I'd forgotten to go swimming – and now it was too late. The realization was terrible – absolute horror. It ended the dream like a crash-landing after a fall – I woke up and my heart was racing. In variations of the dream, it occurred to me that I hadn't gone cycling, hadn't had a bonfire in the garden, had missed the August meteor showers. But by far the worst dream was of missing the group photo: I dreamed we'd forgotten the photo. We hadn't gathered outside the house, put our arms round each other's shoulders, with umbrellas or without, we hadn't got a stranger to take our photo to see the children growing taller and us growing old, to capture us growing old and do something to stop it. We'd missed out on it. Irretrievably – everyone had left. Everyone was gone.

A dream from the midst of life. A weighing-up – chances missed and not missed, things said, not said. The fact that we miss out at all – and we do, we're constantly missing out. But which detail of the dream have I forgotten?

The group photos are still wedged between the frame and the glass of the kitchen cupboard to this day. They're allowed to stay there even though I had to give up the house, have given it up: returned it to the family, back to the old structures.

My father has reclaimed the house, my brother and sister have taken possession of it with their children, my old uncle is still there, and all that is fine, because I've grown old and gone away, because the circumstances have straightened out. The salon is tidy, a family shrine. My father cleaned the cabinet, sorted the dinner service; on festive occasions he lays the table with it. The grandfather clock ticks away.

The piano is tuned, the certificates hang neatly side by side, the room's showpiece is the photograph of the golden wedding. Unlike back then, I know now who the people in the photo are. Like my father, I can tap the faded figures with my index finger and say: my grandmother, my great-grandmother, my great-grandfather, who built stoves in Russia, my great-great-grandmother, who they say was a witch. When my parents celebrated their golden wedding, my father recreated the photograph. My parents' wedding anniversary was also my father's seventy-fifth birthday and presumably the first birthday he ever spent with his whole family, ever endured his family congratulating him on being alive. The idea of recreating the golden wedding photo must have been a product of his compulsion to control and frame everything, to create a situation instead of letting it come and surrendering to it; all my life, my father has been incapable of sitting around and seeing what happens. But above and beyond that, the idea was also consistent, actually lending my parents' unreal golden wedding a centre and almost a meaning.

To this day, I'm amazed that that 4 July dawned, took place, came to an end; it amazed us all. The no-nonsense celebration of a festive date was so breathtaking that we had to accept it; the day overpowered us, a gift given to us, and then it was over. The weather summery, warm and settled, the family arrived in an unusually cheerful state, the grandchildren witty, the table beneath the plum trees as if thought up for another family in another life.

My brother protected by his wife, my sister by her husband, my uncle peaceful and sober, he too allowed to invite women who'd played a supportive role in his life, feeling appreciated and taken seriously. My father wore the only suit he possessed, previously worn solely at funerals. He had written a speech; he asked my mother to read it aloud. My mother read standing, in her best reading-aloud voice, still girl-like in a white blouse, a soft woollen cardigan, very virtuous; anyone passing by would have seen that she didn't remotely understand what she read, that she understood nothing, none of us did. The speech was about my parents. About time, about a measure, about the stuff that keeps things together, perhaps that's what it was about; I was so overwhelmed that I can't really remember it now. It was a piece of my father's inner world, which was obviously utterly isolated, complex and impossible to share, and we accepted that too for his sake, sat still with our heads lowered and listened to my mother's voice as she passed it on to us, at least acoustically. Immersed in the speech, a little anecdote was secreted about my parents' honeymoon – a twenty-four-hour trip, overnight, to the Erzgebirge mountains – on which the owner of the guest house had whispered at them, the morning after their wedding night, that life was nothing but two things: complicated and primitive. There was nothing between those two poles, he muttered, that was all they needed to know, and my mother read aloud that my father agreed with that conclusion to this day. And then we got up and kissed and hugged, went out in front of the house and posed for the photo.

We posed in front of the house according to my father's instructions – just like our ancestors almost a hundred years before, which meant that I, the oldest daughter, sat in the front row in a chair beside my mother, with my sister's twins in front of me on the grass and my son, in the role of my grandmother, on the right-hand edge of the picture, my sister behind, my brother to the left of my father, and so on and so forth, and we did it: we slipped into that time.

Briefly, my father stood next to me and asked whether I found it disturbing to take the place of

Martha, a dead woman's place, and I answered, confused, that it was anything but disturbing; quite the opposite, I found it consoling and in fact – beautiful, and that was how I felt. Unlike a hundred years ago, there was no photographer, no eyes from outside; we set up a timer, remained among ourselves, much to my regret.

Ten seconds, counted backwards.

Done.

The photo of my parents' golden wedding is now on the wall next to the photo from 1927. My father is clearly the central figure, perhaps partly because he looks so very different to usual. He's gazing at the camera the most directly of all of us, his face wearing an expression of conclusive earnestness; accusation, anger and insight, a resistant, strong face from which all – yes, all self-pity and confusion has vanished. My father is looking at the moment, he's pulling it off. His family flanking him, devoted. My mother has lowered her head and is inspecting something small on the grass to the left of her feet; she has turned away. I can't say how I look. My son is smiling. House, trees, sky above us are there, like a hundred years ago. We, in the foreseeable future, won't be.

When I later asked my father why we hadn't taken a photo like this one earlier, on other occasions, he answered without hesitation and with ill-concealed disapproval of my idiocy, my ignorance.

He said: Because it's a final photo.

In a way, I think now, that sentence belongs to my stories. To my writing. I can write more easily about things once they are over, once I know they will be over. Final doesn't mean everything is good the way it is. It merely means that things have somehow come to an end, at which point they have to find themselves anew, start over from the beginning. In *The Summer House, Later* I wrote that happiness was always the moment before. These days, I'd write that happiness is always the moment after – the moment in which you've survived the supposed happiness, got away in one piece, recognized happiness as such and lost it again, let go of it and cast it aside. That's what is final, or to put it another way – that's where I've got to in my writing, and I'm sure it ultimately means the same thing, whether happiness comes before or after.

I've moved Anna the doll in her red dress on her chair; she's now perched on the base of my desk lamp. She's looking at me. I might think she's observing me, but that would be too drastic; she's looking at me a little like she's in a theatre audience. She's looking at a woman who's sitting at a desk, she's watching this woman. Behind her is a card someone sent me from Berlin, a coincidence since I've never spoken to anyone about this text: a line by the director Einar Schleef.

Remembering is work.

The card, the lamp and the doll on the chair look almost like an art installation. I've increased the distance between me and the doll, making her less part of me, more of an object. She knows something that I've cocooned and concealed inside me, and she will keep it to herself. I don't write to deal with this riddle. I write because that's how it's turned out, the riddle merely denoting the way in which I work on my stories, think of them. I write the way I'd dream, were I to dream. I write a first, second and third version of the story. From every version I strike something out, put things back in, take away and repeat and take something else away; and whatever has been irretrievably lost in the last version is what I wrote the story for. Impetus and motive.

It doesn't matter that it is lost – it was there once, and having been there implies an afterglow, a metaphysical condensing. You can think that ridiculous; I don't care – I insist on it. You have to concentrate, you need your sixth sense. The feeling of entering a room that someone has just been in, and they have gone but they've left something behind, a vibe, a specific atmosphere.

Sulphur and dust.

To write stories is to be distrustful. To read is to engage with the story. Every story tells of a ghost. At the end, the centre of the story is a Black Hole, but it isn't black, and it isn't dark. In the best case, it might gleam.

III

IN THE WINTER OF 2020, IN THE FIRST pandemic winter, I moved from the city to the countryside for good, into a house at a safe distance from the village and my grandmother's summer house, like the narrator's house in my book *Daheim*. My family stayed in the city due to COVID. Everything is standing still. I've been in the countryside for almost three months now – alone for longer and more excessively than ever before – and there are moments when it seems as though every connection to the old world has been cut. I feel I ought to watch out that the same doesn't happen in reality; I ought to maintain the floating state between memory and the freedom to remember nothing at all, and take care that the weight doesn't shift to one side or the other. In November and December, with the second lockdown, came a feeling that Turgenev describes in

his novel *Rudin* as 'fallen to the bottom of the river'.*
The world passes heavily over you, full of suffering, sorrow, beauty, but you are below the stream, you hold still there, and because you're holding still you can stay where you are. Life underwater, strangely similar to the feeling described by the narrator of 'The Red Coral Bracelet', life as if underwater, days without bottom. The difference, of course, is that my protagonist in the story is very young and I am old or on my way to being old; evidently, you can be carried by the exact same feeling at very different times in life. The 'Red Coral Bracelet' narrator's feeling in life was my feeling. Thirty years ago. And in my memory, that feeling in life was rather unhappy. That same feeling, now, is almost happy. Is that a comfort? Does it mean anything at all.

There are few people here whom I see and talk to; actually, there's only one. I see Jon. The justification for this restriction is COVID, but ultimately I wouldn't want to see any other people even without COVID; I simply want to see only Jon, and COVID sets up a repeated motif that I yearn for:

---

* Translated by Richard Freeborn (Penguin Books, 1970).

I and another are alone in the world.
Jon and I are alone in the world.

In November 2020, during the days when I felt submerged at the bottom of the river, we spent several afternoons in the local provincial town's palace-turned-museum, where Jon had work to do. He had to select and photograph odd details of the interior that didn't catch the eye at first glance, and we spent hours in the drawing rooms and cabinets and lying flat on our backs on the parquet to spot the hidden messages in the ceiling paintings, the frog in the heron's beak, the god pulling the wind chariot, the exposed breast, bare shoulder turned away. The museum was closed due to the pandemic. No one there but us; we could play at being other people and we did so in appropriate gratitude for the circumstances: in contemplative mode. Three days; we stayed beyond the early break of dusk, and on the last day the nightwatchman almost locked us in. Friday.

He surprised us in the audience chamber, where we were sitting on the window ledges, looking out over the abandoned palace square. He said if he hadn't happened to hear our voices – we hadn't been speaking at all – he would have locked us in unintentionally. He waited politely for us to gather up our belongings and escorted us to the exit; he said he wouldn't have been back until Monday, we'd have had to survive somehow over the weekend.

He said: And the cupboards are bare.

Then he locked the neoclassical portal behind us.

Later, I wrote a short message to Jon. I wrote that I'd have very much liked to have been locked in a provincial palace with him over a whole weekend; I wrote: how regrettable, we would have told each other everything.

Jon often comes back to that. He repeats it – we would have told each other everything. He wants to know what that would have been: everything.

It's an amusing question. It's impossible to tell him what that everything would have been; we both know that disclosure will never happen now. Two days and nights in a palace would have led to a truth that has now gone the way of all flesh, beyond recall; how reassuring to assume that there is always more than one single truth.

Jon doesn't let it go, nonetheless. He says, nonetheless: What do you mean by everything. What did you mean by that.

I could tell him: Well, our obsessions, for instance. You'd have finally been able to tell me your secret wishes, we'd have got to that point in forty-eight hours, you could have staked everything on one card; but of course, I don't say that.

I don't say anything.

December is over, the new year has broken and I rise up from the bottom of the river, back to the others; I need to take a breath after all. Taking a breath leads to speaking. Since the new year began, Jon has been talking much more to me than last year, I've been talking more to him; every sentence we formulate for the other brings an intricate new riddle. The more we try to explain ourselves, the more we misunderstand one another. Like in a fairy tale. Silence is golden, they say.

I ask Jon why that might be.

He thinks for a while, then he actually says: It's because of the ghosts.

I think I know what he means.

One of the things Jon photographed in the palace is a night painting: *The Appearance of the Last Wolf in J*. It is a dark painting. Thick, oily-black, a sole tiny light in the window of a cottage on the far right of the picture. Jon has a thing for wolves and presumably selected the painting because of its title; there was actually nothing to see in it. But then his camera's screen revealed a very different picture: that of an actual wolf, on the far right of the picture but distanced from the house, its ears pricked up in concentration, one paw lifted as it picks up a scent. The cottage too emerged as if out of a gloaming, pastures on the horizon, a ditch, scattered stars; it was not a night painting at all, it was a dusk painting. The lens, as unsparing as it was gentle, salvaged a scene from the black, which was apparently just a coating of soot and grease laid down over centuries – it switched on the light. We were delighted and shocked.

Had that shock won out, Jon might have kept the picture for himself. But our delight was greater, and so he included it in his selection of pictures for projection onto the palace façade, a photographic Advent calendar for the people of the town, a new image every evening for twenty-four days. A daguerreotype of two children with a toy coach and goat from the century before last. A painting of the Three Graces. Dragons from the murals, a portrait of a young girl with coral earrings, a wooden sculpture of a gracious Virgin Mary and child, a garden scene, a picnic on the edge of a forest with a view. All these motifs greatly enlarged, interrupted or underlined by the palace's windows, ledges and castellations. The projection was entitled 'Advent, Arrival and Vicinity' and the scenes frequently featured several people, showed them touching, being together. No music, no additional acoustic or visual stimuli, the palace square dark, the projections static, one main image and every day, like behind the flaps of an Advent calendar, a new small image. More people came night after night and stood outside the palace, which they were not allowed to enter and which, in that last month of a difficult year, arrayed a few of its treasures on its outside walls, made them visible.

Reverence. There was something reverent about people's silent standing.

The wolf appeared on the façade on the evening of 15 December. The picture was projected so that it was loping over the entrance, one paw resting on the window where Jon and I had sat together that November afternoon. The cottage was bent out of shape by the curve of the palace tower, the wolf was alone in the world, the stars rising or setting above it. The audience reacted no differently to the wolf than to other motifs. They lifted their phones and photographed it, as they had photographed Graces and wind gods and taken those photos home with them to show to someone, to forward to someone, to send them out into the world via WhatsApp, Signal, Twitter – the bag from their visual hunt. Had they asked Jon where to find the wolf in the palace, he would have had to pass. It was not visible in the painting; it was protected by the darkness, and not until today have I thought that Jon and I fetched it out from that protection into a flash of light, declaring open season.

And because I'm passing the days with perhaps dubious metaphors like this, I think of Marco, and because I'm thinking of Marco, an evening comes to mind that we spent together a long time ago; it must be more than ten years back. It was just the two of us that evening, and perhaps that's why it comes to mind; it was rarely just the two of us, only at the end when Marco was ill and I visited him at his flat and then in the home. But that evening in Prenzlauer Berg, he was still well or didn't yet know of his illness. What presumably happened is that the others were there at first and later went home, and the two of us ended up staying behind; we never made arrangements in advance back then. We'd go out. Walk down the road, turn right and then left and rely on fate; you could always count on running into someone, somebody from the inner or outer circle of Ada's pack, Ada's family; you'd walk into X on the next corner and Y at the one after that, and then you'd be in the crowd. Berlin was a small city. It was a village and an island.

In the scene that has stayed in my memory, Marco and I were standing outside a bar on Lychener Strasse, a terrible place that afforded itself the affected luxury of a bouncer, who refused to let us in. Perhaps we were too drunk for him. Perhaps he wanted to show off, or the place was full, or Marco hadn't taken him seriously enough – whatever the case, he wouldn't let us in. Late summer, the night not yet cold and no longer warm. Marco debated a while, then he gave up. He let the bouncer be and lay down right in front of the bar in one of the puddles between the paving stones, still crooked back then. He lay flat on his back, spread his arms, pulled up his legs, a contented man; he smiled, he looked up smiling into the night sky above the city, navy-blue and curved like an upturned dish. He nestled up to the paving stones as if the granite were soft. I watched him in amazement, and the bouncer watched him equally amazed, but his amazement gave way fairly soon to disdain, and then anger. He came out of his doorway and said: Get up, man.

Go on, get up. Bugger off. Piss off. Piss off out of here, both of you.

I'd given up smoking a few months previously; it had been very hard work. It was dangerous for me to go out, drink alcohol and abstain from smoking, and I was half-drunk and pretty irritated. The bouncer was smoking. Filter between thumb and forefinger, quick, hard drags, he had to pull himself together not to give Marco a kicking, and when I saw that I took his cigarette from him. I plucked it from between his thick fingers and first puffed at it like a cigar, then I took a drag and smoked it all the way to the end.

Hard to say why I did that. Distraction or self-harm. Or perhaps simply a variation on Marco's design, an unconscious and sibling-like comment; I understood Marco's position, I understood something about it that I couldn't put into words.

The bouncer was too stunned to take the cigarette back from me and the nicotine shot like an intravenous injection into my weaned-off nervous system, into my fingertips and toes; it felt like the poison it was and it felt fantastic, and I took another drag, and another, and Marco said languidly: Ach, just get out of my sight, man, I'm right where I belong. I'm right where I want to be.

Too much for the bouncer, incomprehensible, and he shook his head and actually spat on the ground between us, but that was all he could come up with and in the end he went back inside his bar and slammed the door behind him.

After a while, Marco got up and strolled over to his bike, which he'd propped up against a tree. He angled his head and looked at it, then he threw it around and jumped up and down on it; the spokes cracked, the mudguard broke. It looked beautiful, like a dance, a ritual; he was wearing Doc Martens and a heavy jacket and he jumped powerfully, and in the street-lamp light the dirty puddle water flew in silver and opal droplets from his shoulders, his outstretched arms, angled hands. Ada had told me that, as a child on the way home from school, football, swimming, Marco had always needed to break something, he'd broken off car mirrors, smashed glass, kicked in garden gates, had to destroy something before he got home; no one could stop him. That night on Lychener Strasse, I too did nothing to stop Marco from kicking his bike to pieces; it would never have occurred to me to stop him.

I went home.

The next day was a Sunday and Marco called me early in the morning. He'd had a blackout and he asked whether I knew where his bike was, and I said I'd show him. He picked me up and we walked through the lifeless Sunday-silent neighbourhood to the bar, where the rotting shutters were down and the trashed bike lay slung across the pavement. Marco spent a long time looking at it. I was certain he remembered now but he said nothing, and I said nothing either. Then he picked it up; it was still just about possible to push it and that's what he did, he pushed it alongside himself and we walked a little way and then drank coffee in a Portuguese place with fogged-up windows. We sat side by side at the counter by the window, wiped holes in the fogged-up glass and looked out at the street, watched the occasional passers-by, the pigeons scurrying around between the cars to the dented bike, which was propped against a lamp post. We didn't talk about the bike, nor about the puddle, nor about the night. We were very closely connected that morning; less so before, later never again.

Marco, I think now, was the only person I took to meet my parents, introduced to my father. The fact that I did so must mean I trusted him, unlike all the others. Winter. Marco was working for a carpenter at the time, and my parents were already the last tenants in the building and couldn't get their flat to warm up; Marco had suggested taking some wood over to them. He knew my parents were the last people in the whole residential complex, something that impressed him in an anarchic way; the days of abandoned, vacant flats and squats were long over by then. He knew no more than that, I had never told him about my family's special circumstances. He pulled up outside with a trailer full of wood, lugged it down to the basement and up to the balconies; my father made coffee, behaved sensibly but was also alert, cautious as if Marco were unpredictable, as if he were wild. I watched Marco, waiting for him to notice something he'd find strange; I was certain he'd ask me later about one detail or another. The untidy flat. The chaos in the furniture-crammed rooms, my father's tattered cardigan, his medication boxes, his crumpled papers covered in rows of numbers, his inattention and his tiredness; but he asked me nothing. Either he noticed nothing, or what he did notice didn't surprise him, or it simply didn't interest him. My father pretended to want to know this and that about Frankfurt an der Oder. Marco told him this and that. We had a second cup of coffee with chocolate-coated marzipan, then we headed back to Prenzlauer Berg. It's nothing spectacular but it is spectacular for me, it's a story in the sense of an occurrence: all this occurred. And I never wrote about it until now. And the question is, if I were to write about it, whether I would drag into the light Marco's fragility and vulnerability, his illness – which might have played a large part in scenes like the one on the street that night – the way Jon dragged the wolf into the light at the palace. In the thin-skinned irritability of these silent and withdrawn pandemic weeks, everything has gained greater meaning – the codes grow and turn less comprehensible – and I think that a story's secret is one thing, and a story's wolf is another. Would Marco's fragility be the wolf in a story. Or, put differently – can I tell of the wolf without declaring open season.

Before the pandemic, a year before it, Jon and I had gone on a short business trip together – how cosy to use the word business, which doesn't really come up in a writer's daily life – a research trip to the Oldenburg region. We'd stayed overnight in a hotel on a small-town market square, checked into adjacent rooms in the late afternoon and arranged to meet up for dinner in the hotel restaurant; there were two hours between our arrival and our dinner date. I put down my suitcase, stood in the doorway in my coat, counted to a hundred and tiptoed back out of the room; I wanted to be outside again and alone, walk around the town on my own and look into the brightly lit windows of its houses. Nothing strange about that. We had been travelling together for days so it was natural to need space, and we hadn't agreed on how we wanted to spend the two hours we were to be apart. Nonetheless, there was something of a lie to the way I crept as quietly as possible past Jon's room to the stairs, and I felt caught out when I returned an hour and a half later and he spotted me, since he happened to be talking to the man at the hotel reception. He raised his eyebrows as I entered the lobby, then turned away. The situation was amusing; it was as if we were spies and he had caught me crossing over to the opposite camp. It was actually amusing, but beneath that it was serious. We talked about it over dinner. Briefly. I wanted to distract him from the fact that I'd been out on my own, had eluded our loose agreement to see the place together without discussing it with him, and so I told him a little about my evening walk around the town and he listened. I had walked to the edge of town, through an industrial area and back to the centre, then climbed the church tower

– he listened, bored and clearly distant. He acted as though none of it was worth mentioning; he was right about that. He seemed upset, and when I asked if he was upset he said my secretiveness got on his nerves. He didn't say 'a bit' or 'a little'; he simply said: Your secretiveness gets on my nerves, and I said: My secretiveness is a result of trauma. It comes from trauma, I'm sorry.

I said: I'm the traumatized child of a depressive father, I come from a family of mad people, I have to conceal the myriad symptoms of mental illness from the world, or at least I think I have to.

I said that, or something like it. I added two or three illustrative details, my father self-harming in the psychiatric ward, the suicides, my grandmother's illness; I kept it short. Naturally, I hadn't ever talked to Jon about my family, and he had never told me about his. There was sure to be some abyss or other in his family, perhaps not as obviously as in mine, but whatever the case, he must be familiar with the link between childhood and character; for me, that connection only became clear at that moment. It was only in that provincial hotel that the link between my secretiveness and the darkened rooms of my childhood became clear to me, like a push, at the exact moment when I said it. I must have been angry with Jon to give him the information like that. Or I trusted him. Did I – actually – trust him. I told him something I had never told my other so-called friends, my entire chosen family over all the summers, had never told Marco. In response to his accusation of secretiveness, I told him my secret.

Jon took note of it. He didn't bat an eyelid. He listened to the secret the way he had previously listened to my descriptions of the town's arterial roads, stoically, actually looking as if I'd said something entirely different, and he might have wanted to give me an opportunity to take back what I'd said. To rethink. He looked as though, had I asked him to, he'd have said: I didn't quite catch that.

But I didn't take it back.

And then the food arrived, we ordered a second glass of wine and waited for the pepper mill, the salt shaker, a bottle of still water, please, and then we talked about something else.

Even now, Jon hasn't asked me about my childhood again. Even now, I haven't mentioned my childhood again. But I often think about it. I often think that I told Jon something weighty about myself and that, astonishingly, nothing changed; or at least, any possible change hasn't brought any tangible difference, and I wonder whether that's a good thing or less so. I wonder whether Jon has suppressed the memory of my secret, which was no longer secret from that evening on, and from now on certainly isn't. The idea of him doing so almost amuses me. That passed-on suppression, a dropping reflex; I put a hot coal in his hand and he dropped it.

Would he still remember it now.

Or would he say in genuine surprise: Ach. You told me that? I don't remember it now.

Because: if he remembered, wouldn't he actually have asked, over the subsequent months? Asked questions, cast out a line, how to put it – cast a fishing hook after the secret floating away on the river, caught it, reeled it back in, lifted it out of the black water, struck it over the head and interrogated it. Or is he doing exactly the right thing – accepting the secret and tucking it away. Tucking it away for me. Asking questions wouldn't change anything about the secret, wouldn't lessen its weight. Perhaps it's better to leave these things to stand, not to interrogate them, to leave them as they are.

I'm thinking about it as I sit here at my desk, under the steadfast observation of the doll in the red dress on her tiny chair and under the lamp and in the company of the books stacked up round the computer, beside the bed, on the kitchen table and on the stairs, waiting patiently for me to decide on one of them. For me to get the idea of opening one up, letting one book point me to another, to discover the fragile signs concealed between the pointers.

Coincidence and intuition.

I read Sarah Kirsch, Tove Ditlevsen, Gerbrand Bakker, I read Lars Gustafsson and John Updike and Christoph Ransmayr and I think about writing, and while I'm doing so it occurs to me that I'm writing here almost exclusively about the stories I won't write or haven't written, which is the diametric opposite of my task; nonetheless, or perhaps because of that, it is an attempt at an answer. If thinking in stories means doing two things at once – since writing entails both revealing and concealing – that requires me to hold a straight course between those two poles. Every story is a retrogressive motion towards a beginning, piling up around a centre; piling up not only my own story but also those of others. I seek recourse much more, in fact, to other people's stories, which I read so as to find my own voice, which wouldn't be audible at all without these other voices. This piling-up of writer upon writer, John Burnside tells us in 'Where executives would never want to tamper', creates an atmosphere, creates a sense of moral nourishment which we carry with us, I think, lending all the more clarity in this pandemic year. I spend the days at my desk, particularly the very early day when it's still dark outside, 'no longer and not yet', as Sarah Kirsch calls it, putting a name to this morning darkness for me, just before the sun rolls over the horizon.

I take off my reading glasses and look out, then I put my glasses back on and look at my laptop screen, I take off my glasses often, and I look out of the window for long periods. The room is large, almost empty; now and then I stand up and walk to the room's end and back to the desk.

I drink tea.

I make several pots of tea, replace the tea light in the warmer, burn Japanese incense sticks; I noticeably distract myself with tiny flames. With lighters, matches, smoke. I look at the screen on my phone, switched to do not disturb. I can't resist reading the messages, photos, pictures, videos, greetings, sequences of the lives of others so far away from my isolation, for which COVID is an alibi. From time to time the postman comes, or the woman next door. The dustmen. I read two poems. A page of Houellebecq's *Schopenhauer*, a chapter of Bakker's *Jasper en zijn knecht*, I read Tove Ditlevsen but never during the day, only in the mornings and evenings. Updike too. I eat something. I talk on the phone. I get in the car and visit Jon in his studio in the provincial town, with the view of the palace and the market square, with the view of what I sometimes forget in the loneliness of my outlook over field and sky:

People.

We sit on two chairs side by side and look out on those people – cycling, wearing masks and usually in the rain – and we talk a little, this and that. The kingfisher in the palace grounds. The rising, falling, rising case numbers. How our children are dealing with the pandemic; Jon has three children and a lot to tell me on the subject. This or that book – he prefers Scandinavian writers and shies away from American literature, so I can't talk to him about Updike – the weather, the light, the new year beginning.

Would you like another cup of coffee.

Yes please. One last cup of coffee, yes.

On one of these afternoons – pandemic afternoons, and I wonder about the price to be paid for this antisocial peace in Jon's room while all around us the world is coming unhinged – Jon says out of the blue: We could open up after all. He wants to say: We could open ourselves up after all. Tell each other things, be open, it's a matter of trust in each other and in ourselves. What prompts this capricious suggestion is a photo of my desk in my writing room in Berlin, which I'd dug out from my archive the night before and sent to him on WhatsApp. I'd sent it to him because I wanted to tell him about a picture hanging above that desk and was too lazy to describe it. Jon doesn't know my flat in Berlin. With the exception of my secret, he knows next to nothing about my circumstances in Berlin, and I hesitated to send him the photo: my world.

I ask him what he thought when he saw the photo, and he answers that he was shocked.

Precisely – he hits the bull's eye.

Jon got a shock because I showed him a detail from my world without preparing him, I shocked him with a photo of my desk; that's the right expression for me, I think he's right to be shocked. Appropriate, even though he wants to reformulate the word, confused by my enthusiasm – his shock had been more of a surprise, he says. It's too late; of all possible words, shock is the right one. Every book gives you a shock like that. But it maintains a distance, it has an inherent cautiousness that lessens the shock. The distance is the imagination, your own choice of images. And the movability of the object – I can close the book. Shut it, open it up again and read on to the end. I'd like to think that Jon's way of dealing with my secret, revealed to him in that provincial hotel, is the same as my way of dealing with the secrets of books. When I read a book I take on its secret, I adopt it. And I keep it to myself. Perhaps that was one reason why Jon said we could open up. He actually wanted to say that the shock is temporary and is followed by affection – and then love.

He's quite sure of it.

I say: Do you know how to open up. Do you know how to do it.

He says, determined: I do know, yes.

I say: That's good. Because I don't.

Do I open up when I write a story.

Or do I close up.

Writing a story is torturous, it's hard work to encapsulate the sentence that initiates a story, or it's joyous, entertaining, a gift in the end. And either way – once I open up a story, it's over. I open it up once it has told what I think I know, and then it no longer interests me, in a way. What carries a story is the tense anticipation of a misfortune or an occurrence, a sense of waiting for a widening of the world. Opening up might mean arriving; I'll ask Jon, he knows these things. Arrival – the finale – takes place only outside the story, far beyond its ending. I'd like to contend that all stories have an open ending; the open ending is what makes them stories. The stories I love have open endings. The girl in Carver's 'Why Don't You Dance?', the boy in Hemingway's 'The End of Something', Richard in Updike's Maples stories, the narrator in Turgenev's 'The Clatter of Wheels' – all these characters are left at the end with their hands raised, empty.

How will it go on?

The possibility of opening up certainly takes place inside the story. An allusion that leads nowhere, an insight with no objective, flickers of thought or awareness. The girl in Carver's 'Why Don't You Dance?' tries hard for it – *there was more to the story and she was trying to get it talked out. After a time, she quit trying.* Hemingway puts it in the title, 'The End of Something'. Of something. I think I know what it is that Carver's girl senses but can't name or doesn't want to. I sense what Hemingway's boy means when he says: *It isn't fun any more.* The narrator's horror in

'The Clatter of Wheels', one of the best short stories ever written, is the horror of death, and it remains nameless.

Opening up means dragging that something out of its vagueness, the wolf into the light. Explaining what exactly the something is would presumably mean expelling the wolf. Not explaining makes the wolf safe. Allows it to live.

At the end of my sixth book, the narrator opens the trap beneath the extended roof behind her house. It's unclear what is caught in the trap, even to me; but I do sense it, or in other words – I know it, but I don't have words for it. Whatever it is, it will come out, reveal itself, become visible. The narrator will see it, outside the book, after its ending, and she'll understand it. I will see it. I have seen it. And the reader, if they're a gentle reader, will see it too.

And then?

Opening up is absolutely dangerous. In life, as in writing and in reading, though that danger is delayed in reading. Does Jon know that. Should I point it out to him. Or has he already worked it out for himself.

I spent one of my birthdays in recent years, my forty-ninth, with my father. It was the night before

– we went to see *Death of a Salesman* together at the Deutsches Theater. My father wanted to treat me to a theatre trip for my birthday; I had accepted his gift, although it was clear that I was actually giving him the gift of going to the theatre in my company. No matter. We sat at the end of the fourth row in a sold-out auditorium, for a staging by a young director whose ideas had something pleasantly reminiscent of school plays, characters casting shadows like paper cut-outs, a rotating stage, children's voices from offstage. I'd seen the play thirty years before, in another theatre in the other half of Berlin, and I remembered weeping so many tears that I'd found it hard to locate the exit. What had I been crying over? I sat in the theatre next to my father and kept hold of the thread that might have led to another evening thirty years before, but the thread began to fray, to dissolve. Tears came to my eyes again at the end. Willy's outbreak, his imploring description of himself. *Who am I.* My father was attentive but unmoved; later, he said the actors had spoken too quietly for his taste. As far as I could tell, he didn't cry. His years on the psychiatric ward drove crying out of him, not necessarily forever, but certainly for some time; my father had cried himself out. The audience gave a standing ovation.

We stayed in the empty row for a while. Then we left as well.

It was a warm evening, not late but already dark as we left the theatre. We agreed to drink a glass of wine, get a bite to eat. Even now, eating with my father is difficult for me, aside from the fact that he prefers food that is unpretentious in an absolutely pretentious way, a combination hard to get quite right. We walked up Friedrichstrasse, where one restaurant borders on the next, chip shops, Indian-Vietnamese fusion, kebab shops and trattorias, and my father couldn't decide; one was too crowded, the next too empty, the third too authentic, the fourth too trendy, and eventually we ended up in Keyser's.

Keyser's is a bar on Tucholskystrasse. Nothing special; the special thing about it might be that it's been around for twenty years and hasn't changed at all in that time. An L-shaped room with a wooden bar, seats grouped by tall windows, solidly worn tables, the view of the street perhaps nice: the unrenovated building opposite, the glittering fairy lights above the ground-floor door that leads to a club I used to go to often. Keyser's had a small menu, simple wines and the typical waitress for the scene, dull at first and then suddenly uncomfortably attractive at second glance. We sat down in a corner by the window, ordered red wine; my father flicked through the menu. I'd spent a few nights at Keyser's twenty years before, and countless nights in the building opposite, in the club and the backyard and on the roof with its view of the synagogue dome. People from Ada's chosen family had lived in the building; as far as I knew, they still lived there. I looked up at the windows and felt released from something diffuse while my father worked his way through the menu and eventually made the joyless choice of vegetables and chicken, a heavy meal for that time of day and for my taste.

And what are you having?

Bread and olives.

My father cast me a glance, as though my choice harboured a message to him that had slipped out by accident, a message he had definitely received, however – his reaction a familiar provocation that I ignored; I was old enough not to take the bait. I could let it rest. We got the wine and a bottle of water, we clinked glasses and talked a little about the play, the cast, Arthur Miller, the staging's vanities, the unchanged bar and the building opposite. The conversation was disjointed at first, then improved. When our food came there was too much for my father, as expected, and he put some of his chicken on my plate, and I put it back on his without him noticing, and then he ate it all. We ordered more wine and he told me about his childhood birthdays. Berlin-Zehlendorf, number 13, Waldhüterpfad: his father absent, of course, his mother not home from work until evening; once it was night they'd sit down on the steps at the front of the house and wait for the Allies' fireworks. Fourth of July. My father said he'd thought for years that the fireworks were for him. Just for him, a gift from his mother; the only one, incidentally. He'd been seven, perhaps, when he realized the fireworks had nothing to do with him at all.

He said: Yes. That's how it was. That's how it went.

In between he kept checking his watch, and as midnight approached he got fidgety and started rummaging in his brittle leather bag. There were two guests left at the bar; the barman was rinsing the last glasses, dimming the lights, turning the music down while the waitress chained up the chairs and tables on the pavement. My father said: Getting old is a heroic thing. I don't mean your getting old, I mean mine, which is inextricably linked with yours. Getting old is for heroes.

I said: Is that how you see it.

Yes, said my father, I do see it like that, and if you get old you'll see it like that too, and you'll think of me. It's horrific. It's an absolute imposition.

He bent over his bag again and I realized he wouldn't just be raising a toast to my birthday at midnight; he wanted to lay out a little birthday table for me. I looked at the two people at the bar and the barman; none of them looked over at us. My father took a squashed miniature cake and a saucer out of his bag, making a meal of unwrapping the cake from its plastic packaging and placing it carefully on the saucer. For a moment, the situation felt unbearable. Torturous and embarrassing. I was ashamed. And then that feeling was over; my shame lessened, paled and was suddenly gone. I leaned back and watched him unpacking a candle and pressing it into the cake, unwrapping a newspaper-swathed shot glass and placing a tiny dented bouquet in it, arranged as far as I could tell out of flowers that grew on my parents' balcony.

Horned violet.

Forget-me-not.

Grass.

His hands were shaking. He inclined his head and surveyed it all, pushed the cake forwards a little and then back again; I could see that these tasks made him happy, and I thought my father might be setting a final birthday table for me in Keyser's, might never again wish me a happy birthday.

I thought: We don't know that.

We don't know that.

He placed a wrapped book next to the cake and lit the candle. It was midnight, and he raised his glass, and I raised mine.

Later, we walked through the deserted nighttime centre of Berlin to Friedrichstrasse Station. Tipsy, peaceful; perhaps our father–daughter relationship, the connection we've had my whole life, was at its most peaceful that evening. My birthday had just begun, I was probably relieved to have got the meet-up with my father over with already, and whatever the case: we walked in harmony through the old Jewish quarter, stopping to decipher the names engraved on golden brass cobblestones in the light of the street lamps, reading them aloud:

Efraim Adlerfliegel
Perla Eisig Schächter
Moschek Fraidenberg
Kurt Feuerring

We recited their dates of birth and death, calculated how long they lived, spoke the names of the places where they were born, the camps where they were killed. Perhaps in this speaking of names and dates we let go of our own story, allowed it to be lost and become part of a bigger picture. Witnesses, aware of the historical guilt and oblivious of ourselves, and we were alone on Ackerstrasse, Kleine and Grosse Hamburger Strasse, Tucholskystrasse, and at the same time together and sheltered. And then at Friedrichstrasse Station, and I let my father take his train first – he stood in the carriage, half-smiling as the doors closed and the train took him away, and I waited a long time for mine in the other direction, to the north-east of the city, and I went home to celebrate my birthday with my chosen family.

Yes.

Scenes like that.

In his studio in the provincial town, Jon tells me about a dream he dreamed as a child. He dreamed, he says, that a horse was looking in through his window – not a big deal, Jon says, but in his dream he tried in slow motion to grasp the thought that his bedroom window was on the third floor and so it was impossible for a horse to look in, and if a horse was in fact looking through the window, that must mean the horse was abnormally large, and if it was abnormally large, that meant the world had gone off the rails, had gone crazy.

And I, Jon says, had gone with it.

My father has recurrent dreams of a lioness coming into his bedroom. Into the little room in the little flat on Kantstrasse, clearly a lioness, and she lays her big soft paw on the door handle, she opens the door with her lion's paw.

I dream that I'm on a bicycle, a tiny live bird tied firmly to the handlebars, a fluffy wren, a winter bird. The city in the light of the bicycle lamp. Tarmac. The tiny bird suffering visibly.

In January 2020, before the pandemic is to permanently change the structure of time and memory, I go to stay with my editor Jörg Bong in Brittany, to finish my sixth book. I stay a week; unlike previous edits, when I didn't fall ill until afterwards, this time I fall ill beforehand. Extreme migraines, nausea, fever, absolute weakness; I lie in bed in the guest room and think I might be about to die. What could it be – the pain of separation, detachment, an expression of fear and failure. Starting over again, something divides up, reassembles itself. I am sick for three days. Then I feel my way out of bed, out of the room, and we make a cautious start at editing; I drink tea, eat an apple. We get the intro done. A walk in the afternoon. In the evening we drive into town and go to a restaurant; I eat a piece of white cheese and a walnut. I'm allowed to be slow, Jörg is patient; we finish the book at the end of January; it is still called *Trap 1* at this point. We leave at dawn. Jörg takes me to the station in Rennes and I catch a train to Paris, change from Montparnasse to Gare du Nord. Local transport workers are striking and I don't want to take a taxi, so I spend two hours locked in traffic on a replacement bus more crowded than anything I've ever experienced. I am squeezed between two women, pressed up close to each other; it's not possible to keep a distance between us and after a while we admit it to ourselves, give in, surrender ourselves. I rest my chin, then my cheek, on the shoulder of the woman in front, the woman behind me droops heavy and warm against my back; it's a little like a performance, it's a capitulation. A borderline experience; looking back to what was to come, it was almost painfully beautiful.

In February the virus appears in Germany, and my son says: If it comes to Berlin I'll move to the countryside; he's sitting on the crackling wicker chair at his father's kitchen table as he says it, and snow is falling outside. Lockdown in March. No one moves to the countryside. My son goes up to the attic with his girlfriend and his best friend and sets up a table and chairs in the former laundry room there; they lug old army coats out of crates, sit underneath the skylight and light candles in wine bottles, and later they say they'll never forget those nights; the image of the children in the attic has a questionable poetry to it that confuses and embarrasses me. There are days when I walk the stairwell with a bottle of disinfectant, wiping down door handles, banisters, light switches and doorbells. Outside, the traffic slowly ebbs and then comes to a stop, and my son's father and I sit on the balcony for the first time; it was always too noisy and dusty otherwise, and we drink beer and watch the moon rising above the roofs of the psychiatric hospital opposite. It's so quiet that we hear the nightingales singing in the trees. The district in northern Germany where my house is closes its borders. Jon writes a message – deer are sleeping in the garden, rabbits are coming into the house.

Spring begins.

I meet my parents in Sophienstadt Cemetery, bringing along a folding chair and a thermos flask of tea. We sit in a socially distanced triangle in the cold May sunshine, them side by side on a bench, me opposite on my chair. The meeting place in the cemetery is my father's suggestion; the pandemic is his triumph. It confirms what he's always known: life leads to death, and death is suffocation. We will grab at nothingness, no one will hold us. The pandemic manifests the distance he has always felt to others. It justifies him being alone. It establishes it and exhibits it. My mother is my father's hostage. She's dressed up for our encounter, wearing a loop of wooden beads and child-like red shoes. Whenever she unconsciously leans closer to me my father pulls her back. We don't hug, we don't kiss. We take a socially distanced walk around the cemetery to the grave of Max Stirner, the philosopher who set his cause on himself,* and I think that my father has set his cause on himself too and that perhaps I do the same, whether I want to or not; that's how it's turned out.

---

* *Der Einzige und sein Eigenthum* (Otto Wigand, 1845); *The Ego and His Own*, translated by Steven T. Byington (Benjamin R. Tucker, 1907).

Then we part ways.

In June the case rate falls, the district reopens its borders and I go to my house by the sea. I weed the grass from between the paving stones, mow the lawn, carry the sleepy fat spiders out one by one; I haven't been here for so long. My brother and sister's double wedding on Wangerooge Island is cancelled. My parents stay in Berlin and my father no longer leaves the house. He permits my mother to leave the flat twice a week and for special shopping trips, orders food online and stows the deliveries on the balcony for forty-eight hours to decontaminate them before he puts them away. I sometimes think about calling Dr Dreehüs, but then I remember my emotional toolkit; I think I know how to use it. I don't call Dr Dreehüs. The summer house remains empty, only my old uncle goes in and out of his three rooms, and there are afternoons when I cycle over there, put up a chair in the garden and sit in the sun. On the spot where we took our group photos, the ones with my friends, the ones with the family for my parents' golden anniversary. I sit there for a long time, trying to understand that both these times are over, and then I return the chair to the shed and cycle back to my house.

In September, once the summer is over and the autumn wave of the pandemic begins to descend, I go to Berlin one more time; it will be the last time for a while, which I don't realize. It's presumably a good thing I don't realize it. My brother and sister were in Berlin two weeks before, stayed in my flat and left before I arrived to reduce contact. My mother sent me a photo of them on my parents' balcony, between miniature olive tree and oleander. I haven't seen my brother and sister for a long time; they look good in the photo but their smiles are either melancholy or guilty. My sister has her hands crossed in her lap, my brother is sitting next to her, leaning slightly towards the camera; in front of them, on the table with the blue tablecloth, is a bowl of bright-red cherries.

Over the phone I ask my mother when the photo was taken.

My mother clears her throat. Then she says: Oh, that was last week, before your brother and sister went back to France and Switzerland.

For a moment, I don't understand her answer at all. Incomprehensible.

My brother and sister without masks on my parents' balcony, in my parents' flat, which no one has been allowed to set foot inside since the start of the pandemic; how can that be?

My mother explains, audibly embarrassed. Oh gosh. It just turned out that way. They were nearby, they wanted to go for a walk, and then they just came over instead, knocked at the door with masks on, wore their masks inside the flat, only took them off on the balcony. To eat a cherry. It makes no difference if you sit together in the park or socially distanced on the balcony. They didn't stay long. Half an hour, maybe. If that.

My mother says: You can come and visit us too now. You can sit on the balcony. The case numbers allow it.

I say: Who says that. Who says the case numbers allow it. Is that what Papa claims. I can't imagine he does.

My mother says: For once, that's what I claim.

I take the train to Kantstrasse, putting my mask back on before I knock. My mother opens the door. I've brought flowers, snapdragon, thistle, chamomile. We stand there, no longer knowing how to do it: visits, we've forgotten the rules of visits in the space of six months. Then my mother takes a step towards me, I extend the flowers away from me, she takes them from me, she smiles. Neither of us says anything. She gestures at the bedroom door, ajar, behind which my father is playing chess on his computer, has been playing chess continuously for six months, usually against opponents from Korea, Singapore or India, then she beckons me onwards and I walk past her down the short hallway, through the living room and onto the balcony. Dizzying. No time to look around, to register the room where my parents have been locked down for months. An impression of a track, a trail leading past the table to the balcony door and out onto the balcony, a palpable sign that my parents have been treading certain paths in their flat even more frequently than usual. I'm certain the floorboards are worn. I can't look. I swim across the room, reach the balcony like a shore, I drop down onto the little bench in the far-right corner where my brother and sister sat too; I take off my mask, at long last.

The blue tablecloth on the table, a single cup, no saucer, no spoon for my coffee. I'd considered bringing cake and then abandoned the idea, convinced my mother would have baked a cake to celebrate my visit; she's been baking constant loaves of bread, at least, since the pandemic started. She clearly hasn't baked a cake. She clearly hasn't managed to track down any cherries either. My mother fetches my father out onto the balcony; they both stand on the threshold and gawp at me. Then they sit down opposite me in the far-left corner, my father so visibly pleased to see me that it hurts. My mother has cut his hair; he looks like an old child. She told me he checks the case numbers on the internet every morning and is disappointed when they don't rise, don't double, triple, increase tenfold.

My father wants the whole world to suffocate.

I say: There probably isn't any cake, is there. Or maybe a biscuit. Just a dry biscuit.

My mother blanches, her hands flying up. She looks at my father, and my father says: I'm afraid there's no cake. He says it questioningly, pretending not to understand why I'm enquiring after cake.

He says: I'm afraid there's no biscuits either. But there's coffee. We've made coffee.

He gets to his feet and leaves the balcony, and my mother says: I'm sorry. Oh, I'm so sorry. We didn't even think of cake; her voice sounds appalled.

I wish I could take back the question about cake; it's becoming clear this is all too much for my parents, cake belongs to a completely different world, a world lost and gone. But it's too late.

It's too late.

My father comes back with the coffee pot, pours

coffee with what I see as a deliberately unsteady hand into the cup, which I've placed at his end of the table, and I take it back after a period gauged by some logic or other. My parents don't drink anything. They've already had coffee, perhaps. I don't ask for milk or sugar. Their eyes are fixed on me.

How are you, my father says.

Fine, I say.

The plants lovingly tended by my mother, growing on my parents' lightless balcony, actually growing past my parents, around them or over them. Olive and oleander, hydrangea with gigantic leaves but not a single flower, a miniature lemon tree with no lemons, dominated by stonecrop, basil and lavender, lemon balm, sunflowers on swaying stalks tied to wooden sticks with parcel string. This balcony, between these plants, is where my parents have spent the whole summer.

It's quite poignant.

Right, says my father, what shall we do about your brother and sister's wedding.

My siblings have moved the double wedding planned for Wangerooge in May to France in November. They're still planning a party but they've only invited half the number of people, though that's still forty. My parents have been wracking their brains for weeks over whether to travel to the wedding or not. How to travel. If at all. By train, first-class. With me, on the back seat of a rented people carrier, me driving them across Europe, wearing masks at all times. By plane. Or, better, simply not at all. In optimistic moments, after nine in the evening and his second glass of wine, my father says you only get one wedding, especially a twin wedding, and of course he'll attend. My mother says she's going, no matter how, she's definitely going, COVID or no COVID. But then they waver again. They retreat, they say they have to weigh it up.

I say: If you want to go, I'll drive you.

My father says: Why does this wedding have to happen right now. In November. In this terrible year, what's driving your brother and sister to get married in this exact year.

I say they asked their fortune-teller, and the fortune-teller picked the date.

My mother raises her shoulders but she's far too slow; I've said the word *fortune-teller* and I can't take it back. Ultimately, I know it'll lead to disaster. I said it deliberately. I'm punishing my parents for the forgotten cake, the lack of cherries.

What fortune-teller.

My father looks at my mother, leaning towards her in case she hasn't understood him.

What fortune-teller.

My mother says she knows nothing about it.

Of course she knows about it. She knows full well that my brother and sister consult a fortune-teller for major life decisions and take the fortune-teller's answers at face value.

My father looks at me, he says: What are you talking about then.

I say, I'm not talking about anything, I'm answering your question. You asked me why the wedding has to be in November of this terrible year, and I answered your question. The wedding will only be possible in November.

He says: You're telling me your brother and sister let a fortune-teller decide their lives. In this case, all our lives. Dictated by a fortune-teller.

I say: That's right. They let Mona Astra dictate to them.

My father looks back at my mother and my mother turns away. His expression now, I can't put it any other way, is full of hate. None of us say anything for a while.

Then he says: Do you know what you're telling

me. What you're doing to me by letting me know. You might as well say your sister's a streetwalker. Your brother's the head of that new Nazi Party. I couldn't say which would be worse for me. I couldn't say. A fortune-teller. God in heaven. A fortune-teller suggesting a wedding in France during a pandemic winter.

I pick up my cup, sip my coffee and put the cup back down. I can sense my heartbeat; I feel like crying.

I say: There are people who get through life with fortune-tellers, and others who add up numbers and take comfort from Gauss and Kepler.

My father says: I won't let you tell me anything about Kepler.

I say: I didn't tell you anything about Kepler.

In vain. He gets to his feet and leaves the balcony, slamming the door behind him.

My mother and I sit together a little longer. There's nothing more to say, really. There's nothing more to say here. We listen to the arriving and departing trains, their triadic signals wafting over from Savignyplatz Station, we sit in silence. I've had a good summer, and perhaps it's enough for my mother to know that, to see it in my face.

She says: That's it, then. That's it for our trip to France.

She sounds almost relieved.

I say: Yes, that's probably it. It's probably a good reason not to go.

She says: I'm sorry your father is the way he is.

I say: You don't need to be sorry. Not any more.

My mother gives the balcony door a cautious push open and we both listen into the flat, but the flat is silent. My father's retreated to the bedroom. He won't show himself again. He's punishing all three of us.

I say: You've got to look on the bright side, anyway.

My mother says: We do.

I put my mask back on and walk through the cool, shady living room; out of the corner of my eye I can see the flowers my mother has arranged on the table, the thistles, the glow of the chamomile. She knows more about flower-arranging than anyone else. I walk along the hall, I stop at the door and touch my mother briefly on the elbow. Down in the courtyard I turn round and look up at the kitchen window, and she's standing there and waving.

Like she always does.

Outside on the street it's surreally warm. It smells of tarmac summer, of artificially flavoured smoke from the shisha bars. People are crowded close together outside restaurants, families and couples, drinking white wine, their voices cheerful and relaxed, gratified by the late-summer warmth, the onset of dusk, the sun sinking behind the tall buildings. My siblings get married two months later without a single guest, officiated by a priest in a mask; they'll be allowed to take off their masks for the wedding kisses, and a day later the whole of France will be in a hard lockdown. Mona Astra was right, in her own way.

Write that down.

That comment of my father's – just write that down.

He means 'Tell that story' – because it's funny, peculiar, crazy or unique, because it's a story that in a figurative sense tells a different, larger story. But something acute happens here for me, something explicitly personal – I can't just tell a story, I have to bring myself to safety first, I have to start by defending myself. I ask myself when I'll ever feel like writing another short story, under these circumstances. Whether I'll ever want to think of a story at all, under these circumstances. I've written down the situation on my parents' balcony but the pandemic is too close, it illuminates it too dramatically, there's something sobering about it. Not magical. That's how it is now – right in the middle of the pandemic. Perhaps I'll feel differently once we've got through it and survived, once it's over and pupates and alters in our memories, once I'm allowed to alter it in my memory. For me to write the story of my visit to my parents' balcony – and it is a story, I know it is – the pandemic and the related story between me and my parents has to have ended.

In that first long, surreal COVID winter of 2020, reliant on myself and my halfway-functioning communication with Jon and growing increasingly earnest and strained from being alone, I sometimes have a sudden yearning for Ada. Jon visits me. It's a Sunday. For days now the news reports have been warning of snowstorms, cold and the onset of a catastrophic winter; the snow never comes, stormy winds, that's all, and I feel disappointed. Jon is relieved; he doesn't like it when the weather determines his life. I think Jon doesn't have the faintest idea about weather. We sit by the window and look out on the storm, watch the crows flung across the field by gusts of wind, the crows surrendering, firing across the black soil. We drink tea. Jon lit the candles on the table while I made the tea in the kitchen, and that act of lighting seemed extremely personal, almost intimate. He's brought back Enquist's *Downfall*,* says he couldn't find any connection to us, which is strange because I didn't give it to him for any possible connection, I'd just quoted a line from the book – *it cannot get simpler than that. But who says it has to be simple* – and Jon was interested in the line, that was all. I had reread the book, which I'd loved dearly thirty years ago, before I lent it to Jon; unlike back then, we now have the internet, and I'd looked up Pinon online. My mental image of Maria and Pinon's face was replaced by an online depiction, which felt significant and had ultimately torn the secret out of the story. *Express my face in breaths.* Pasqual Pinon was born in Mexico in 1889 and performed at Texan fairs; he had a growth on his forehead, made up as a woman's face. Yes. Jon says he couldn't find any connection but he still enjoyed the book. He asks me what I'm reading right now, and I say *Snow Country* by Kawabata, which isn't true. The storm waxes, the light wanes. Jon is still talking about opening up; he wants to tell

---

*   Translated by Anna Paterson (Quartet Books, 1987).

his story, he wants to tell me something about his complicated relationship to women. By telling me, he wants to justify why he does this and doesn't do that, he wants to create a connection. He doesn't get far, of course. He gets caught up in insinuations and then hands over to me, asks me to tell my story, asks me to tell him something about my complicated relationship to men.

I refuse. I say I don't have a complicated relationship to men at all.

He says: Yes, you do. And you write about it. You write it down, don't you.

Puzzled, I say: No, I don't write it down. That's exactly what I don't write down, I've never written down my so-called stories with men.

He says: Aha.

I get the impression we're talking at cross purposes, skirting the nub of the matter. It seems that way to him too; he gets up and stalks around the room, and it's at that moment that I have a sudden, crystal-clear yearning for Ada. For her face and her attitude, her exact and yet sloppy way of laying a table; I have a devastating yearning for the sight of her shirt collar over a rough brown wool sweater, that way of wearing a shirt under her sweater, neat and yet with an insinuation of possible dissolutions of boundaries, of total excess. The conversation with Jon has something exhausting about it. My age has something exhausting about it. I'm yearning for Ada because I'm yearning for certain years, for a back then, for something approximate. December Sundays and we'd meet up in Ada's apartment, the flat she'd moved to after her separation, the children still little, Ada's son very little and my child a little boy, and Ada's daughter a beautiful little girl, and we'd sit round the table with the children listening to the *Christmas Oratorio* and sticking shapes cut out of wax disks onto candles. The children's candles were decorated with stars and hearts, the adults' with more complex, geometric forms, words and symbols; Marco was the most immersed of us all.

The Floater.

He had a project he called 'The Floater', a perpetuum mobile, an egg rotating inside a ball and floating around the world, driven by a neverending energy. It was an incomprehensible and presumably pointless project, absolutely unscientific, a poetic image, an idea. He cut the construction of the floater out of the wax sheets, stuck interlocking rings, gold and silver, onto his candle, and the children watched him reverently, holding their breath as if they thought he might stop and leave if they spoke to him. Once the evenings set in we'd drink wine, and Ada would have put a goose in the oven – almost in passing, as always; those were the years when we roasted geese without mentioning it; what did we ever mention at all. We certainly didn't have conversations like this one between Jon and me, twenty years later. Our time together had something, I'd like to say animal-like about it, and despite that it was conventional, conservative – it contained everything we knew, everything we'd been taught: the rituals of an Advent Sunday. Candles, marzipan and mandarins, huge bouquets of amaryllis and holly, pine needles on the parquet floor and that music, eating together, making things together with the children, and even though something about it remained little more than stage props and deception, it was still Ada who made it possible, who insisted on giving us structure and connection.

And I think of all that while Jon paces the room behind me, and that's why I have this almost disturbingly strong yearning for Ada: because the connections are slipping away from me, because apart from me there is no one left to make and maintain them.

With age, writing shifts away from a centre once thought secure, from a serenity once taken for granted. It shifts away from thoughtlessness. It becomes sharper, and yet less. Perhaps it ebbs away. Or it returns to that centre and tries again, tries again from the beginning.

As laborious as talking to Jon is, it is certainly necessary, and in retrospect the years with Ada and the others seem like a second childhood, one long, last sleight of hand, an evasion of adult life, the gravity of the situation and the whole thing. Everything Ada did added up to a picture. Her child's scribbles on the kitchen wall, the knick-knacks on the windowsill, in spring the wilted forsythia twigs in the vase on the table by the open balcony door, Ada leaning against it and smoking, one arm wrapped round her waist beneath her chest, left elbow resting on her right wrist; we were so practised at keeping each other at a distance. And when I listen to Jon and me, our incomplete comments and insinuations, I'm not at all sure which attitude is the right one. Neither one nor the other? In the end, it seems, it all comes out the same; you are – Turgenev again – alone like a finger.

How alone is a finger.

Once the evening has fully set in outside, Jon

leaves. He doesn't ask me about my work on this piece; he doesn't dare. But he would like to have another try at a collage together, like back when we were travelling in the provinces and I told him my secret, he says, and he, knowingly or not, did what you have to do with secrets: he hid it.

He sets off, and while he's putting on his coat – in a story, that *while* would be an important detail – he asks me again if I could imagine putting writing and drawing together, letting them speak to one another.

I say I could imagine that.

I really can imagine it. Even though it's hard work, I'd like to do it and I think perhaps that's one way for us to make progress. I write something and Jon draws, we exchange one enigma for another and thus expand the enigmatic circumstances in the world.

Then the only question is, Jon says, who starts. Not me, I say, I'm definitely not starting.

I'm dreaming.

I dream of my mother, who sends me a note that says she's not doing well, she's seeing stars, having problems with her balance and can't concentrate properly. She writes that she's read somewhere that if you feel that way you should just lean against a wall, and that's what she's doing, it's sure to help, and anyway my father will be right back, he'll be back in the early hours of the morning. That's not enough for me in my dream – leaning against the wall and waiting for my father – and I look for my mother and find her in bed in our old Neukölln flat, wrapped in a blanket on the side where my father always used to lie. The room is in a state of disrepair, all its colours brown, ochre, sepia, my mother perhaps as old as I am now. She smiles. She says: Oh, I'm all right again, it's nothing, don't worry; but I wake up as if from a nightmare.

I dream that my father and I have lost our way in a run-down high-rise estate on the edge of town; we're looking for a way out and find a dilapidated subway beneath the street, which I suspect is almost too much for my father – he seems to have surrendered his entire authority to me. Ragged, shady-looking characters appear at the bottom of the stairs, then move aside and let us through; my father clearly comes across as fragile. No point in jostling such a fragile man. He links arms with me, inserts his right arm beneath my left elbow the way my grandmother used to, in real life. In the middle of the subway is a large, dazzlingly lit supermarket, and we stand by a freezer and watch an exceptionally fat woman shovelling artichoke hearts into a flatbread, then she goes to the till, her shopping trolley pulled by a black dog that looks like a llama. My father's eyes on the woman, then on my face, on me – as if I were conjuring it all up out of a dubious hat, as if he wanted to say: So this is how you see the world. I break off the dream. I get the impression I'm breaking it off, it's too close to me.

My father's coming too close to me.

What comes to mind, Dr Dreehüs liked to say on the rare occasions when I presented him with a sparse dream image, what does it make you think of.

Sometimes slightly irritated, as if the question were superfluous, as if I ought to have figured out by that point how the whole thing worked. What comes to mind about your dreams? The prolonged heaviness that comes over me with that question, an absence. The shadowed consciousness. The shady path to an uncertain place, actually similar to the beginning of a story: What comes to mind with this line, which one character says to the other and which seems to me to mean something monumental beyond the banal – how do I get to that sentence, how do I find it.

What comes to mind about these two dreams about my parents.

I'm amazed by the archives of my memory. The sunken flat in Neukölln, my parents' folding bed with its brown-cord upholstery, the sewing table instead of a nightstand, the tiled heating stove with its niche for an icon, inside it a porcelain bullfinch that my grandmother exchanged for flour during the war and later got back again in exchange for more flour; it was my grandmother who once lay on that side of my parents' bed, wrapped in a brown blanket and silent, as if floating, on a Sunday visit; and then she'd gone into hospital and died there.

I'm worried about my mother. Less so about my father; my conflict with my father is shaped by other things, and anyway I've always had to worry about him. I see myself standing by the supermarket freezer with him, and it comes to mind that I don't ultimately know what distinguishes dreams from reality. The dream is equal if not superior to reality in impressions of light, colour, love, fear, helplessness; there are dreams, rare but nonetheless, in which I've dissolved for sheer love, in which I've flown, and I remember my fear from the doll's house dream to this day. It's existential. Interwoven with all my years, still here. It comes to mind that I might not dream too little at all – perhaps I'm dreaming all the time. It comes to mind that it might be, after all, the way I read the torn-off note pinned to the wall in the bay window, *and our little life is rounded with a sleep.* Ten years later, I feel exhausted gratitude towards my father for the fact that he left it to me to be the last in the flat, to close the door, Pandora's box, and to throw the key in the Landwehr Canal on my way home, on my way back to the hard work of my so-called own life. But perhaps I only dreamed that note; it's actually too kitschy. The whole situation is kitschy, the abandoned rooms, the grand piano, the tattooed removal men, the dragon – nonsense, meaningless, and either I dreamed it or I made it up, like all the rest as well. My Russian grandmother, the bread soup, my father in a Queen of the Night costume, the puppet theatre, my bed behind the puppet theatre, a bed like in a gulag, which I must have read about, and in the gap between the bed and the plywood wall a shrunken apple, a crust of bread. A line my mother often said to me – you're exaggerating, Judith. You're exaggerating. I always wanted to know what it's like to eat paper. The paper with the code written on it that you must never betray, what's it like to put it in your mouth in a moment of great danger and swallow it, and did I make it up that I did it, or did I do it and am I still.

In the direct and the figurative sense.
I made up a cat for myself, a grandfather's pool table, a psychiatric hospital, the torturous waiting for a nurse to come shuffling when I rang the bell outside the closed ward at the beginning of visiting hours. A lighthouse keeper on an island, a house by the sea, those summers and an Ada, a Marco and me. I dreamed the wolf onto the castle's façade. Running into Dr Dreehüs in the bar at night, the cigarettes and the gin and tonic definitely dreamed, I dreamed of an analysis, a whole pandemic: made up.

What exactly is the difference between making up, dreaming and exaggerating. The actual thing about a dream is not the content or the plot; it's the feeling with which we dream it, the material in the sentient, haptic sense. That material remains when we wake up.

In my previous book, *Daheim*, the narrator talks on the phone to her daughter, who is in a place that remains vague. Desert. Or water. All that exists, this daughter says, is what you're experiencing right now, and every explanation for it is made up and only exists once you formulate it. The narrator, who lives in a house like the one where I'm sitting at my desk right now, looking out at the cloudy grey morning, is me. And she's a dream image. I dream her, and she dreams me. She's a sister in spirit, I obviously made up a story for her, I obviously – to put it in Dr Dreehüs's terms – altered and distorted it all so much that nothing is correct any more, yet everything is true.

I don't have a daughter. I have a son; I don't have a big brother but I do have an old uncle. I tell Jon: You're not in this book, and he says he's relieved to hear that, and I know what he means, but I don't know whether Jon's absence in this book is a cause for relief or rather something to be mourned. It doesn't matter whether dreams are life or life is dreamed, doesn't matter whether a story is invented, true or only half-true, made up or real – it doesn't matter at all. The houses are important, and the rooms, quadrants of your life's stages, the inner structures and the possibility of leaving these houses and their interior worlds and of returning to them. *I'm here in the house*, Carver writes in a poem, *and I want to try again*. I suspect it's that which comes closest to writing, to life.

Trying again.

The cover of the book *The Yellow House* shows the yellow house, its windows, sills, guttering, flower boxes, the gabled roof and the door; the door is ajar, and a little girl slips through the gap into a dark room. Slips into a house, but at the same time into a cave, or rather: into a casing, a hollow space, into a chamber within a chamber within a chamber.

The soul of a story.

The soul of the immortal Koshchei, hidden in a pin in an egg inside a duck inside a hare inside an iron box beneath an oak on the island of Buyan far out at sea, hidden outside his body, and he'll only die if that pin is broken. Broken against his own brow. It seems to me as if the picture of the girl on the threshold of the yellow house and the threshold of understanding, of the way to that box, that egg and that island, is significant. I'm as close to that girl as I am to the taciturn wooden girl on her tiny chair underneath my desk lamp – she has eaten paper, chewed it and swallowed it, that much is certain. The stories I've told here about writing are different to the short stories I write, partly because a story nearing its end simply takes on a life of its own, no matter what I wanted at the beginning. Behind the unlocked door to a story there is always someone who takes me by the hand, pulls me in, closes the door behind me.

Locks it.

Right. Back to the beginning.

Who am I, where do I come from, to what extent can I shift away from the beginnings, am I allowed to forget them or do I have to write them first and then be allowed to forget them. I'm not sure, I typed into a long-gone computer in Wewelsfleth twenty-five years ago. Not really sure. That's astounding, I think now; it seems so right to me, and now too, here and now, I'm:

Not really sure.

But on one of the long walks with Jon on the unusually timeless first fragile days of this year, a Sunday walk, fields in the mist, Canada geese and Nile geese by the water and the sun a glassy disc, I ask him: How did you spend your morning, what have you done so far today, and he answers: I pruned the sloes.

Why am I so sure I'll write a story in which that answer will feature. Why am I absolutely sure of it. What is intertwined with those four words? What is it about those words. It might be that after all these years they *are* linked to something that goes above and beyond me, something that has left everything personal behind. Releases me.

A question, an answer.

The word *sloes*.

The early morning, as I sleep while Jon prunes the sloes, the hard, thorny branches, the frost on the branches, the still day, and I'm asleep. And I was dreaming. And I am dreaming.

MANY THANKS TO OLIVER VOGEL, WITHOUT whom I would not have written the Frankfurt Poetics Lectures.